Go ahead and scream.

No one can hear you. You're no longer in the safe world you know.

You've taken a terrifying step . . .

into the darkest corners of your imagination.

You've opened the door to . . .

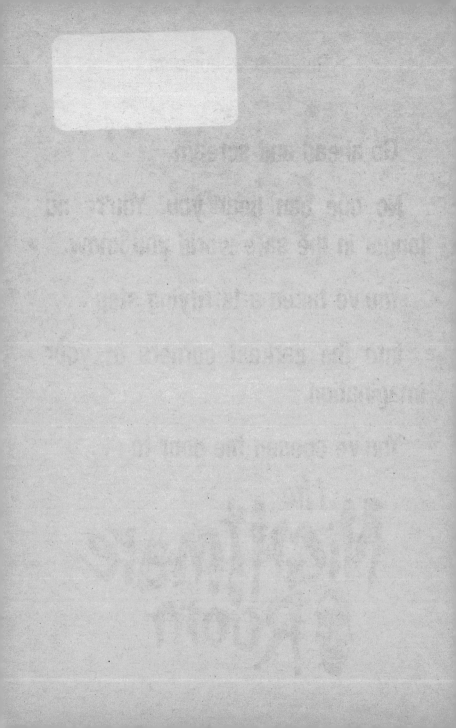

Read all the books in

the **NiGHtmare Room**

series by R.L. Stine

Scare School

R.L. STINE

AVON BOOKS

An Imprint of HarperCollinsPublishers

 PARACHUTE PRESS

Scare School

Printed in the United States of America.

For information address:
HarperCollins Children's Books,
a division of HarperCollins Publishers,
1350 Avenue of the Americas,
New York, NY 10019.

Library of Congress Catalog Card Number: 2001117192
ISBN 0-06-440909-0

First Avon edition, 2001

AVON TRADEMARK REG. U.S. PAT. OFF. AND IN OTHER
COUNTRIES, MARCA REGISTRADA, HECHO EN U.S.A.

Visit us on the World Wide Web!
www.harperchildrens.com

Welcome . . .

Hello, I'm R.L. Stine—and that's my friend Sam Waterbury over there on the sidewalk. Sam is staring at his new school, and he doesn't like what he sees. The old building looks more like a prison than a school!

A big sign says "Welcome to Wilton Middle School." Sam has no idea that most people call the place by a different name. They call it *Scare School*.

You see, something is waiting in the halls for Sam. A creature who is about to give Sam a real education. A creature who exists only in . . . *THE NIGHTMARE ROOM*.

Scare School

"AAAIIIIEEE!"

I let out a scream and heaved my backpack against the wall.

Mom spun around from the kitchen sink. Dad jumped up from the breakfast table. "Sam, what is your problem?" he called.

"The stupid backpack zipper is stuck again," I said.

I knew what was coming. Another lecture about holding my temper.

I counted to five under my breath. Mom was a little slow this morning. She usually starts the lecture by the count of three.

"Sam, you promised," she said, shaking her head.

"I know, I know," I muttered.

"You promised you would work on your temper," Dad said, walking over to me. Dad is very tall and broad like a middle linebacker. His friends all call him *Giant*.

I dragged the backpack up from the floor and tried the zipper again. "I said I would try to keep it together at my new school," I said.

"You wouldn't be starting at a new school if you didn't totally lose it at your old school," Mom said.

She gave me the hard stare. I call it the Evil Eye. It made her look like some kind of dangerous bird, like a hawk or a buzzard or something.

"Like I don't know that!" I snapped.

"Easy," Dad warned, raising one of his huge, beefy hands.

"I know, I know. I got kicked out of school, and you'll never forgive me," I said angrily. "But I didn't start that big shoving match. Really. It wasn't my fault."

Mom let out a long sigh. "Haven't we talked about blaming others for your problems, Sam? You had to leave your school because you were fighting. Because you can never back down from a fight. You can't blame anyone else for what you did."

"Yak, yak," I muttered. I finally got the stupid backpack zipper to move.

"Don't say 'yak, yak' to your mother," Dad scolded.

"Sorry," I muttered. "Sorry, sorry, sorry."

Maybe I'll have that word tattooed on my forehead. Then I won't have to say it. I can just point.

Dad took a long sip from his coffee mug. He had his eyes narrowed on me. "Sam, I know you're tense about starting a new school."

I glanced at the clock. "Tense—and late," I said.

"Oh, my goodness!" Mom cried, placing her hands on her cheeks. "We completely lost track of the time. Quick. Get your jacket. I'll drive you."

A few seconds later, I was seated beside Mom in the Taurus. I stared out at the gray November day. Most of the trees were already bare. The whole world appeared dull and washed-out.

The car roared as we rocketed down the narrow street. Mom drives like a NASCAR driver. The houses sped past in a blur. I pulled my seat belt as tight as I could.

"A fresh new start," Mom said, trying to sound cheerful. She hadn't brushed her curly red hair. It stuck out in all directions over the collar of her brown car coat.

"Mmm-hmmm," I muttered.

I didn't want to say anything. I had my fingers crossed, praying that I could get out of the car without hearing another lecture.

"I know you're going to do really well at Wilton Middle School," Mom said. She squealed to a stop

3

halfway through a stoplight.

"Mmm hmmm." I kept my gaze out the window.

Suddenly, Mom reached out and squeezed my hand. "Be good, okay, Sam?"

Her sudden touch shocked me. We're not a real touchy-feely family. We're not constantly hugging each other the way families do on TV.

Once in a while, Dad will slap me a high-five. That's about as far as we go.

I could see Mom was serious. And worried.

I swallowed hard. "I'll be different," I told her. "No problem."

She pulled the car to the curb. I stared out at my new school.

As I climbed out of the car, my chest suddenly felt kind of fluttery. My mouth was dry.

I really *am* nervous, I realized.

Of course, if I had known the terror that was waiting for me inside that building, I would have been a lot *more* nervous!

I would have turned and run and not looked back.

"Sam, your saxophone," Mom called from the car. "It's in the trunk—remember?"

"Oh. Right." I did forget.

She popped the trunk, and I pulled the big black sax case out.

I hope this school has a good band, I thought.

I've been taking sax lessons since I was barely as tall as the sax. I played in the jazz band at my old school. And some friends and I used to hang out and play in my garage.

Everyone says I'm really talented. I love to play. I love the idea of being able to make all that noise and make it really *rock*.

"Sam, what are you doing? Daydreaming? Don't

just stand there. You're late," Mom called.

She squealed away from the curb. Made a U-turn onto someone's front lawn. Then headed back for home.

I balanced the backpack on my shoulders. Moved the sax case to my right hand. And stared at my new school.

What a gloomy sight.

My old school was brand new. It was modern and bright. And it had four separate buildings, and every building was painted a different bright color.

My old school was very outdoorsy, like those California schools on the TV shows. We walked to class outside. And there was a huge lawn with a little pond where everyone hung out and relaxed.

Wilton Middle School wasn't like that.

It was a square-shaped old building. Three stories tall with a flat black roof. I guess it had been built of yellow brick. But most of the bricks had faded to brown.

On one wall of the building, the bricks were charred black. It looked as if a deep shadow hung over that wall. I guessed there had once been a fire there.

The grass in front of the building was patchy and choked with tall weeds. A barbed-wire fence ran around a small playground on the side. A U.S. flag on top of a flagpole snapped and flapped in the strong wind beside the entrance.

It doesn't look like a school, I thought. It looks like a prison!

I climbed the three steps and pulled open one of the front doors. The door was heavy, hard to pull open. The glass in one of the windows was cracked.

I stepped into the front hall and waited for my eyes to adjust to the dim light. A long, dark hall stretched in front of me.

The walls were painted gray. Rows of black metal lockers made them even darker. Only about half of the ceiling lights worked.

I took a few steps. The *thud* of my shoes broke the silence of the empty hall.

I glanced around, searching for the office.

Where is everyone? I thought.

Yes, I'm a few minutes late. But why isn't there anyone in the hall?

I'm assigned to Room 201, I reminded myself.

Is that on this floor? Or is it up one floor?

I began walking quickly down the hall, my eyes moving from side to side as I struggled to find a room number.

I passed a glass display case with one dust-covered basketball trophy. Above the case, a small blue-and-yellow banner read GO, GOLDEN BEARS!

Two classrooms were dark and deserted. I searched for room numbers but didn't see any.

Maybe they don't use this floor, I thought. Maybe all the classes are upstairs.

Lugging my sax case, I made my way down the long hall. The only sounds were the scrape of my shoes on the concrete floor and my shallow breathing.

The sax case began to feel heavier. I switched it to my other hand. Then I started walking again.

I turned a corner—and heard footsteps. Very light and rapid.

"Hey!" I called out. "Is anyone there?"

My voice sounded hollow in the empty hall.

About three doorways down, I saw a flash of movement.

A figure darted out into the hall.

An animal. Only two or three feet high.

He had his back to me. He didn't seem to know I was there.

His skin was greenish yellow, covered in patches with green fur. He hopped like a bird, stooped over, on two legs.

Skinny arms hung limply at his plump sides, nearly to the floor. He had small pointed ears that stood straight up on a hairy green head.

What IS this thing? I wondered, staring at its back. A giant green rat?

But then he stopped. And slowly turned.

His mouth gaped open as he saw me.

He hissed at me. A frightening, angry sound like a snake about to attack.

And then he turned all the way around. And I saw him . . . saw him so clearly.

And let out a gasp of horror.

The green rat creature—*it had a HUMAN face!*

"NO!"

A cry escaped my lips.

The creature hissed at me again. He pointed a long, skinny finger at me—and whispered in a raspy, dry voice.

"You're IT."

Then he spun around—and loped off on all fours. His long tail scraped the floor behind him.

A second later, he disappeared around a corner.

I blinked several times, as if clearing my sight. The hall stood empty once again.

"What *was* that?" I muttered. Was it an animal? If it was, how could it SPEAK?

The light in the hall was so dim, the walls so dark.

Did I really see that thing?

My heart pounded. Should I chase after it?

Did anyone know a strange animal was loose in the school?

I made my way to the corner and glanced both ways. Long, empty halls. No sign of the creature.

A number above the corner room caught my eye. Room 201. A hand-lettered sign beside the door read MR. KIMPALL.

Breathing hard, I pulled open the door and lurched inside. The room was filled with kids, and they all turned to look at me.

I didn't make a graceful entrance. I stumbled over my saxophone case, and my backpack fell off my shoulders.

Several kids laughed.

Mr. Kimpall, a short, middle-aged man with a shiny bald head, jumped up from behind his desk.

"An animal!" I gasped. "There's some kind of weird animal out there!"

The laughter cut off. The room became very silent.

"Animal?" His expression puzzled, Mr. Kimpall came toward me. He was nearly as short as the sixth-graders in the class, and toothpick-thin.

He wore a yellow turtleneck sweater pulled down over straight-legged black pants. His bald head glowed like a pink Easter egg under the big ceiling lights.

"An animal? In the hall?" he asked.

I nodded, still breathing hard. "It was about this high. And it had a tail—"

"Did it see you?" a blond-haired boy in the back row asked.

"Y-yes," I stammered. "It hissed at me and—"

A few kids gasped.

"You're in major trouble," the blond kid said.

Mr. Kimpall raised a bony hand. "Quiet, everyone. Stop." He turned to me. "Everyone likes to tease the new kid," he said. "Don't pay any attention."

Mr. Kimpall smiled. "You must be Sam Waterbury," he said. He shook my hand. His hand was smaller than mine, cold and kind of wet. But his grip was hard as steel.

"I told the class you'd be joining us today," he continued. "I saved a desk for you. Right over there by the window." He pointed.

"But—but—" I sputtered.

He put a hand on my shoulder and started me on my way to my desk. I could see he didn't want to talk about the creature I'd seen.

But I wanted to know. That thing was so ugly and weird, I wanted to know what it was.

I opened my mouth to ask again. But then I remembered my promise to my parents to be a good boy. A perfect angel.

"Don't argue, Sam."

"Don't fight about things, Sam."

"Don't make trouble."

So I dragged my sax case and my backpack to the empty desk by the window and dropped into the wooden chair.

Mr. Kimpall had moved to the front of the room. He had to jump to sit on the edge of his desk. "We're talking about verbs today, Sam." He pointed to a list of words on the chalkboard.

"Can anyone give me an *action* verb?" he asked.

A boy with short spiky brown hair raised his hand. "Tripped?" he said.

Mr. Kimpall narrowed his eyes at him. "Use it in a sentence, Simpson."

"Sam tripped over his music case," Simpson replied, grinning.

Several kids laughed. Mr. Kimpall laughed, too.

I could feel my face turning red.

Is this kid Simpson some kind of troublemaker? I asked myself. Maybe he'd like to trip over my fist!

"Come on, people. Let's give the new kid a break," Mr. Kimpall said, still chuckling. He asked for some other action verbs.

I sank low in my seat. I couldn't really concentrate on the class. I kept picturing that green creature in the hall, hissing at me. Pointing at me.

I gazed out the window. It was still a gray, gloomy morning. The sky had grown even darker. A few raindrops pattered against the glass.

Maybe it was some kind of school mascot I saw out there, I thought. Someone in a costume.

But it didn't exactly look like a Golden Bear!

Mr. Kimpall droned on. Now he was asking for *passive* verbs, whatever they are.

He hopped down from the desk and began to make a list of verbs on the chalkboard.

When I heard the sound, I thought at first that he had squeaked the chalk really loudly.

But then I realized I was hearing a girl's cry from out in the hall.

A cry that grew to a scream of terror.

Several kids yelled out. Mr. Kimpall dropped his chalk and turned to the door.

The door swung open, and a girl came staggering into the room. She was tall and lean and had straight black hair that swept down the back of her purple sweater.

"Tonya—what's wrong?" Mr. Kimpall asked, hurrying over to her.

She was breathing hard, her round face as red as a tomato. Without saying a word, she raised her blue backpack.

She held it in two hands because it was in two pieces.

"Look," she choked out, waving the two pieces above her head. "Look."

Mr. Kimpall swallowed hard. He went pale. He looked like a lightbulb with eyes.

"It went for my lunch!" Tonya cried.

Mr. Kimpall pulled her to the corner.

I stared at the backpack pieces in her hands.

What on earth had happened?

The bag looked as if it had been *chewed* in half!

"Let's try to stay calm," I heard Mr. Kimpall whisper to Tonya. They stood eye to eye. He stared hard at her, as if trying to tell her something with his eyes.

"Calm, okay?" he whispered.

"But—" Tonya started to say.

He took the shredded backpack from her and tossed it behind his desk.

Mr. Kimpall continued to stare her down. "We have a new boy in class," he told her, speaking through gritted teeth. "We don't want to upset him— *do* we?"

Her face still red, Tonya lowered her eyes to the floor and didn't reply.

Upset *me?* I thought.

He doesn't want her to upset *me*?

What's going on in this school? Why is Mr. Kimpall acting so strange?

He had his hands on her shoulders and he was talking to her softly. After about a minute, Tonya walked to her seat in the front row and sat down.

Mr. Kimpall stepped back to the front of the class. "What a busy morning," he muttered.

He glanced at me. "It usually isn't this exciting around here, Sam."

A few kids chuckled. But most remained silent.

I wanted to ask a thousand questions. About the animal in the hall. About Tonya's shredded backpack.

But Mr. Kimpall quickly went back to his verb list on the chalkboard.

The morning dragged on. I couldn't wait for the lunch bell to ring. I was desperate to talk to Tonya.

I needed to know what had shredded her backpack. And why Mr. Kimpall didn't want her to talk about it in front of "the new boy."

Finally, a loud buzzer went off.

Everyone began packing up, preparing to leave.

"Have a good lunch," Mr. Kimpall called. "I'll see you this afternoon."

I left my sax case and backpack at my desk and hurried after Tonya.

The hall was jammed with shouting, laughing

kids. Lockers slammed. One guy was bouncing a soccer ball on his head. Two boys were tossing a milk carton back and forth, keeping it away from a third kid.

I lost Tonya in the crowd. Then pushing my way past a group of girls in blue-and-gold team sweaters, I caught up to her just outside the lunchroom.

"Hey, what happened to your backpack?" I asked breathlessly.

She was half a foot taller than me. She blinked at me. "Are you the new kid?"

I nodded. "Yeah. Sam Waterbury."

"Hi," she said. We had to move out of the way. We were blocking the door. "I'm Tonya Black."

"Your backpack—" I repeated.

She turned and waved to two girls down the hall. "Did you bring your lunch?" she shouted to them.

I couldn't hear their answer. The noise in the hall was too loud.

"Tell me what happened," I insisted. "What happened to your backpack?"

She shrugged. "It's your first day. You really shouldn't ask me about it."

"But I really want to know!" I shouted. "Why did you scream like that? Why did you look so frightened?"

"Please," Tonya begged, backing away from me. She glanced tensely up and down the hall.

"Please—I can't tell you," she said. "Just drop it—okay? Drop it—before you get us both in trouble!"

"Give me a break," I said. "I don't get scared too easily. Tell me—"

But she darted into the lunchroom.

I'm not the kind of guy who just gives up. I followed her into the lunch line. "Tell me," I said. "Did it have something to do with that green creature I saw in the hall?"

Her mouth dropped open. "You—you *saw* it?"

I nodded.

"Oh, wow," she muttered, shaking her head.

"Answer my question," I insisted. "What happened to your backpack?"

Before Tonya could say a word, I heard the thud of footsteps. Then I felt a hard bump, a slap on my back from behind.

The creature had returned!

No.

Not the creature.

With a gasp, I turned—and saw that kid with the spiky brown hair—Simpson.

"How's it going?"

He grinned at me. He had kind of a dopey grin. His two front teeth were crooked.

He had brown eyes and a short, snubby nose. I spotted a tiny silver ring through one earlobe. He wore a black sweatshirt over faded jeans, torn at both knees.

"Whoa. They've got fried chicken today! Excellent!" he exclaimed as the line moved forward. "The fried chicken and the pizza are the only good foods. Everything else in this place is garbage."

"We didn't have fried chicken at my old school," I said. "Everything we had was garbage."

I turned back to Tonya. But she was already carrying her tray to a table filled with girls.

"Hey, how come you changed schools in November?" Simpson asked.

I scooped a big pile of mashed potatoes onto my plate. Then I reached for a piece of chicken.

I snickered. "Well, actually, I got kicked out of my other school."

He stared at me. "Really?"

"Yeah. Really," I said.

"It wasn't my fault," I added quickly. "Some other kids started a big fight in the gym. And I'm the one who got blamed."

I paid for my lunch and followed Simpson to a table. I sat down across from him and gazed over his shoulder at Tonya's table across the lunchroom.

She was talking rapidly to the girls at the table, gesturing with her hands. I wondered if she was telling them about what happened to her backpack.

Simpson lifted a chicken leg to his face and bit into it. "Not too many fights at Broadmoor," he said, chewing with those big front teeth. "It's a pretty quiet school."

And then he added, "Unless you look for trouble."

What does he mean by that? I wondered.

I shook salt onto my potatoes. "What kind of guy is Mr. Kimpall?" I asked. "Is he strict or what? He is such a little shrimp!" I laughed.

Simpson didn't laugh. "He's okay, I guess," he said. "He's not too strict. But he's always popping surprise quizzes on us."

"I hate that," I said.

Simpson jumped up. "I forgot to get a drink." He hurried back to the front counter.

I dug my fork into the mashed potatoes on my plate. Suddenly, I felt really hungry.

I had been too nervous to eat breakfast in the morning. But now my stomach was growling and complaining.

I shoveled potatoes into my mouth. They tasted buttery and salty on my tongue. Really good.

I shoveled in another big heap of potatoes.

I started to swallow. But stopped when I felt something move.

Something prickled the side of my mouth. Something scratched my tongue.

Something is moving inside my mouth, I realized.

Something *alive*!

"Aaaaggggh!"

I spit a gob of potatoes noisily onto my tray.

And stared down at a fat black beetle crawling over the potatoes.

I felt something prickle my tongue.

I spit again—and another big beetle flew out of my mouth, onto the table.

"Uggggh." I felt sick. I started to gag.

I saw another shiny insect poke out from the pile of mashed potatoes on my plate. Then another one.

"Oh—gross!" I choked out. I could still feel the prickle of the fat bugs inside my mouth, all down my tongue.

My stomach lurched again. I gagged.

I stared in disbelief as more shiny black insects swarmed over my food.

My stomach heaving, I jumped to my feet.

"You finished already?" Simpson returned to the table, carrying a milk carton.

"Bugs—" I rasped. "My food—"

He lowered his gaze to my tray. "Excuse me?"

"I've got to tell the cook," I said. "The food—it's crawling with bugs!"

A smile spread over Simpson's face. "You're kidding—right?"

I pointed to the pile of potatoes. "They—they—"

The bugs had vanished. No sign of them.

I grabbed my fork and poked it into the potatoes. No beetles. Frantically, I spread the potatoes over the plate. Then I picked up the plate and peered underneath it.

No. No bugs.

I turned the plate upside down and let the food drop onto the tray.

No bugs.

"You're weird," Simpson said, squinting hard at me. "I don't get the joke."

"It—it wasn't a joke," I muttered.

But what *had* happened here? The beetles had been real. I hadn't imagined them. My potatoes were swarming with them.

How could they have disappeared so fast?

Why weren't any other kids complaining about bugs in their food?

Simpson raised a chicken leg to his mouth and began to chew.

My stomach began to heave again. I spun away and started to jog to the lunchroom door.

"Hey—your tray!" Simpson called after me.

I turned back. "We get in major trouble if we don't return the trays," he explained.

I picked up the tray and carried it to the counter. My legs felt shaky and weak. I was kind of dizzy. I could still feel the prickle of the bugs on my tongue.

I started to set the tray down—and saw a piece of yellow paper clinging to the tray bottom.

I pulled it off. It was folded up.

I unfolded it. Turned it around so I could read it.

And stared at the message scrawled in red ink:

READ MY LETTER: WHO WILL DROP FIRST?

I found a boys' room a few doors down. Inside, I pressed my forehead against the cool tile wall and shut my eyes.

I could feel the blood pulsing at my temples. Taking a deep breath, I forced my heart to stop racing.

When I opened my eyes, I saw that I was still gripping the yellow piece of paper. I raised it to my face and squinted again at the scrawled red letters: READ MY LETTER: WHO WILL DROP FIRST?

I read it again and again. What did it mean?

Was it meant for me? Or had I picked up the tray with the message attached by accident?

WHO WILL DROP FIRST?

Was it some kind of challenge? Some kind of threat?

Was it written in some kind of code?

I jammed the note into my pants pocket. Then I washed my face with cold water.

I made my way upstairs. I searched for Tonya and Simpson. I needed one of them to explain to me what was going on.

But I couldn't find them. The halls were nearly empty once again. The buzzer rang for the start of the afternoon classes.

Mr. Kimpall greeted me with a smile. I saw that I was the last one to return to the room. He closed the classroom door behind me.

"I hope you all had an enjoyable lunch," he said.

I stopped halfway to my seat. I turned and opened my mouth to tell him about the bugs swarming from my potatoes.

But the teacher spoke first. "Sam, I'm afraid you have to leave us now."

"Huh?" I let out a startled gasp.

What had I done? Did I do something wrong?

"The school band practices after lunch on Mondays, Wednesdays, and Fridays," Mr. Kimpall continued. "I guess no one told you the schedule. You need to get up to Mr. Kelly in the band room as fast as you can."

A sigh of relief escaped my mouth. I picked up my

saxophone case and hurried out.

Mr. Kelly, the band instructor, greeted me at the door to the band room on the top floor. "How's it going, kid? Did you get lost? First day isn't exactly a piece of cake—is it!"

He was big and gruff and talked out of the side of his mouth in a raspy, deep voice. He wore a baggy gray sweatshirt over loose-fitting khakis. He reminded me more of a football coach than a music teacher.

The room was big and high-ceilinged. A row of windows looked out on the back of the school.

About twenty kids sat in three rows of folding chairs behind music stands. They were warming up their instruments. A short, red-haired boy stood behind a snare drum, pounding out a frantic rhythm.

Mr. Kelly led me to the center of the room. "This is Sam Waterbury, everyone. Sam plays heavy-duty sax. When he auditioned for me last week, I knew we had someone who could help our band—big-time."

A fat kid with a tuba blasted out a rude sound.

Several kids laughed.

"You can leave your case over there," Mr. Kelly instructed me. "Then take a seat next to Teri, the clarinet player." He pointed to a blond-haired girl in the second row.

I unpacked my sax and put it together. I pushed the mouthpiece into place and slid the strap over my back as I walked to my seat.

"Hi," I said, sitting down next to Teri. "How's it

going?" I licked the mouthpiece and pushed my fingers down, testing the pads.

She flashed me a short smile. She had awesome green eyes. "That sax looks pretty new," she said.

I held it up. "Yeah. It was a birthday present."

Her eyes locked onto mine. "Well, you'd better get a good lock for the case," she said.

I stared hard at her. "A lock? Why?"

She shrugged. "You're a new kid in this school, right?"

I nodded. "Yeah. So?"

"Well, didn't they tell you *anything*?"

"No," I replied. "No one told me anything, Teri. Why do I need a lock on my sax case?"

It took her a long time to answer. Finally, she whispered, "You'll find out . . . soon enough."

After school, I found Tonya waiting for me in front of the building.

The clouds were low and dark. A few raindrops fell on my shoulders.

Tonya didn't see me at first. She appeared tense. She kept twisting a strand of her straight black hair around a finger.

When she turned and spotted me, two circles of pink darkened on her cheeks. "Follow me," she whispered.

She led the way to the street. She didn't say anything till we were away from the school.

Our shoes crunched over the wet dead leaves that covered the patchy grass. We stopped beside a thick and gnarled old oak tree.

Tonya glanced all around, as if making sure no one was spying on us.

"What's going on?" I asked again. "Why are you acting so mysterious?"

"There is something you should know about this school," she said. She spoke just above a whisper.

A van filled with kids rumbled past. The horn honked. I couldn't hear what she was whispering.

"Tonya, what are you talking about?" I asked eagerly. "What should I know?"

She glanced around again. Then she leaned close to me and whispered. "It gets kind of dangerous here—especially for a new kid. The new kid is always *It*."

A gust of wind shook the old tree. Cold rainwater sprinkled down on us from the bare limbs.

I shivered. I suddenly realized I had run out of the school without my jacket!

I knew I had to go back for it—but not now. First, I wanted to hear what Tonya had to say.

"But—what does that mean?" I asked.

She pushed her black hair over the collar of her coat and turned to the street. "An imp lives in the school building," she said softly.

"Excuse me?" I cried. "A *what*?"

"An imp," she repeated. She shuddered and wrapped the coat tighter around her.

I stared hard at her. "You mean, like a gremlin?" I asked. I don't know why, but for some reason, I laughed.

She spun toward me. "It isn't funny, Sam," she snapped. "It isn't funny at all."

I backed away a few steps. The wind blew fat leaves over my shoes, around the legs of my jeans.

"You mean the green animal-thing I saw in the hall this morning?" I asked. "The one Mr. Kimpall wouldn't talk about?"

Tonya nodded. "He's an imp. He lives in the school. He does horrible things. Everyone is terrified of him. The kids and the teachers, too."

I shivered. I tried to kick the wet leaves away, but they clung to my jeans.

"In the lunchroom," I said. "I started to eat, and bugs crawled out of my potatoes."

"That was the imp," Tonya whispered.

Two girls rode by on bikes. She waited for them to pass before she spoke again.

"He has all kinds of special magic," Tonya continued, her voice trembling. "And all of it is evil. Putting bugs in your food—that was just one of his jokes. If he wants to, he can really hurt you."

I squinted at her. Was she really as frightened as she looked? Or was this imp thing a joke?

Yes. Of course. It's a joke, I decided.

A joke the Broadmoor kids play on all the new

kids to make them look like idiots.

"Tonya," I said softly, still studying her. "Imps aren't real. They're made up. You know. Imaginary. They're only in fairy tales and things."

Her dark eyes bulged angrily. "You *saw* him— didn't you? I didn't make him up, Sam. You saw him!"

"But . . . that was a puppet or something," I said. "I know what you're doing. You're playing a joke on the new kid. Slip some bugs in my potatoes, dress someone up in a furry green suit. It's all to scare me. I get it."

Tonya's expression turned angry. "I'm not playing a joke, Sam. I'm trying to help you. You're the new kid. He always goes after new kids."

"Because . . . ?"

"Because he has to show you that he is the boss," she answered. "He has to show you how powerful he is, and how weak you are. He has to defeat you. He has to make sure that you won't stand up to him. That you won't challenge him."

"And what if I *do* stand up to him?" I asked.

Tonya frowned and shook her head. "Don't be a jerk, Sam. The imp has too much power, too much magic. We all do whatever he wants. And we pray if we keep him happy, he'll leave us alone."

I blinked several times. This was all too much to take in. I suddenly felt totally dizzy.

"And the teachers know?" I asked.

Tonya nodded. "The teachers are all terrified of the imp, too. You saw how scared Mr. Kimpall was. He didn't even want to mention the imp to you."

"Why don't the kids tell their parents about the imp?" I demanded. "If the parents knew—"

Tonya grabbed my arm. "Don't say a word to your parents!" she cried. "If the imp finds out about it he'll go berserk! He'll go nuts if anyone reveals the secret! No one has ever told. We all keep quiet."

Yeah, sure, I thought. Sorry, Tonya, but you've gone too far.

I know why you don't want me to tell my parents. Because you don't want to ruin the joke.

She let out a sob. "I don't even want to think about what the imp would do to all of us if a kid was stupid enough to tell his parents!"

She's a good actress, I thought. But I'm way too smart to believe this stuff.

The sky turned darker as the clouds thickened. The street became silent. Most kids had left for home. Another strong gust of wind made the bare trees creak.

"So . . . the imp is going to challenge me because I'm the new kid?" I asked.

Tonya chewed her bottom lip. She nodded but didn't reply.

"He's going to give me a really hard time?" I asked.

Tonya nodded again. "I wanted to tell you all of this earlier. But it isn't good to talk about it in school.

The imp can hear everything you say."

She glanced back at the school. "I'm not supposed to tell you anything. You're supposed to find out by yourself. The imp wouldn't like it if I helped you."

She shuddered again. "It might make him *really* angry."

She really thinks she's fooling me, I thought.

Well, I can put on an act too.

"This whole thing makes *me* really angry!" I exclaimed. "Why should I be terrified because of a little-green-man running around the school?"

"Sam, stop—" Tonya warned.

"I'm *starving*!" I cried. "I didn't get to eat my lunch because of that clown!"

"Sam—!" She clamped a hand over my mouth. "Stop! Don't let him hear you!"

"Maybe it's time someone taught this imp a lesson," I said. "Maybe I'll show him he can't keep pushing kids around!"

Tonya shrank back, her face tight with fear. "Sam—please!"

I wanted to burst out laughing. But somehow I kept a straight face.

Did other kids fall for the little green man joke? Did other kids shake and quake in fear?

So someone slipped some bugs into my potatoes. That was supposed to make me believe in imps? I didn't think so.

"I'm going back into that building to teach the imp who's boss!" I shouted. "I'm going to pound him. I'm going to *waste* him!"

"You—you're crazy," Tonya whispered. "Listen to me, Sam."

But I pulled away from her and stomped toward the school. Rain pattered the ground. I felt the wet drops on my head and shoulders.

I turned at the front door and saw that Tonya was still staring after me.

"Sam—don't!" she called.

I gave her a quick wave and stepped into the school.

I'm just going to get my jacket, I thought. I'm not going to look for a fight with an imaginary creature.

I tugged off my backpack and carried it in front of me as I made my way down the long corridor to my locker.

I heard teachers' voices in a classroom down the hall. Some kind of after-school meeting.

Two janitors in gray uniforms nodded as they passed by me. One of them pushed a large vacuum cleaner on wheels. The other carried the vacuum cleaner hose, coiled around him like a giant snake.

I turned the corner—and stopped.

Halfway down the hall, along the long row of lockers, I could see one locker door standing open.

The locker at the end.

Mine?

I struggled to remember: Did I leave it open?

No. No way.

The locker door moved. I heard a scraping sound. A soft thud.

I could feel my muscles tighten. My breath caught in my throat.

Someone was in my locker.

"Who's there?" I called. "What are you doing?"

Taking long, rapid strides, I hurried over to the locker.

Grabbing the side of the door, I tugged it open all the way—and let out a cry of shock when I saw the imp.

I stared hard at him. No way was he some kind of puppet. Or a kid dressed in a costume. He was definitely an imp!

The creature had his head down as he bent over, searching the floor of my locker.

But as I swung the door open, he jumped upright—and spun to face me.

I stumbled back. And stared at the green creature. His fur-thatched head, his pointed ears fringed with hair, his cold, dark eyes. Human eyes.

"My jacket—!" I choked out.

He wrapped my blue denim jacket around his slender shoulders. He was so short—three feet tall at the most—that the jacket dragged on the floor.

His green lips pulled back in a cold, unfriendly smile. He hopped out of the locker and opened his mouth to hiss at me again.

But before he could make a sound, I grabbed for my jacket with both hands.

The imp danced away.

My hand caught the jacket collar, then slid off.

"Give me back my jacket!" I screamed.

"*Hee-hee-hee.*" The imp let out a high, shrill giggle and danced a little jig. He pulled the jacket open, then closed it tightly around him.

Teasing me.

Daring me to come get it.

His bare feet, fringed with green hair, slapped the hard floor. His dark eyes flashed merrily.

His grin made me even angrier. "Give it back!" I roared.

I dove for him. Wrapped my arms around his knees in a perfect football tackle.

I went down hard. Landed on my chest on the floor.

"Ooof!" I felt the breath knocked out of me.

My hands flew up—and the imp jumped away.

Free from my grasp, he pulled the jacket around him and started to run.

"*Hee-hee!*"

"No way!" I shouted. I stumbled forward on my knees. Reached out and grabbed for the bottom of the jacket.

I missed the jacket. But my hand wrapped around something round and firm.

His tail!

"YAAAIIII!"

The creature uttered a shrill yelp as I tightened my hand around his smooth green tail—and pulled.

He danced and kicked, but I held on.

"Give me my jacket! Give me my jacket!" My voice came out in a harsh rasp as I struggled to keep my grip on the creature.

In a rage, he spun around, hissing and coughing.

He raked the air with long fingernails. Then he shot his hands forward, trying to scratch at my face.

With a gasp, I ducked away. I had both hands around his tail now. I jerked it hard, up and down. Pulled with all my strength . . .

And it tore off in my hands!

"EEEEEEEEEEEEEEEE!" He howled in pain and fury.

I jumped to my feet and held the long tail up above my head.

It gave a final snap, as if alive. Then it dangled

limply in my hand.

"*Give it! Give it!*" the creature screeched in a raspy, hoarse voice. He shot his hand out, trying to grab the tail from me.

But I spun away, pulling it out of his reach.

My entire body shuddered. "Give me my jacket, and you can have the tail!" I choked out.

"*No deal! No deal!*" the imp rasped. "*Give it!*"

He leaped again.

Again, I jerked the tail away from him.

Hopping up and down, he let out a furious cry—and spit in my face.

The hot gob of spit slid down my forehead and burned my eyes.

"OHH!"

I opened my mouth in a cry of pain. Reached up to wipe the stinging goo from my eyes—

—and let go of the creature's tail.

It bounced between us on the floor.

We both dove for it at once—and cracked heads.

"*EEEEEEEEE!*" Screeching at the top of his lungs, the imp staggered back.

My head throbbing, my eyes burning, I grabbed the tail. Shoved it into my open locker. And slammed the door.

"Now give me my jacket!" I cried.

The imp stared up at me, his green face twisted in fury.

"You'll pay!" he rasped. *"You'll pay with your LIFE!"*

To my surprise, he turned and scooted away. The bottom of my jacket scraped the floor behind him. The sleeves flapped wildly, dangling at his sides.

I mopped hot saliva from my eyes and face with the sleeve of my T-shirt. My skin itched. My eyes still burned. Tears dripped down my cheeks.

But *no way* was I going to let that green creep run off with my good denim jacket.

Still half blind, I lurched after him.

I could hear his bare feet slapping the hard floor around the corner.

Wiping my eyes, I chased him. Made the turn—and stopped.

I blinked several times, trying to see in the dim hall light.

Where was the imp?

Where did he go?

And then a figure came moving toward me from out of the shadows.

I took a deep breath. Tensed my body. And prepared to fight.

I blinked again. It took me a few seconds to realize the figure moving toward me wasn't the imp.

I was gazing at a kid I had never seen before. He was moving slowly, hands in the pockets of his straight-legged khakis.

"Whoa." Startled, he stopped several feet from me.

"Where did he go?" I demanded breathlessly. "Did you see him?"

The kid narrowed his eyes at me. "See who?"

"The imp!" I cried. "The imp! He ran this way. I heard him! He—he has my jacket!"

The kid scratched his short brown hair. He had a round face, sort of chubby. His body was sort of round, too. He looked like a teddy bear I had when I was four.

"I didn't see him go by," he said. "I was meeting with Miss Kinley in her room back there." He pointed down the hall. "I just got out."

I stepped past him and jogged to the end of the hall. I looked both ways down the back hall.

Nothing moving.

No sign of the creature.

"I'm Tim Poster," the kid said. "You're the new guy, right? I'm in the fifth-grade class next to Mr. Kimpall's room."

"Hi," I said. I didn't want to stand there and chat with the kid. I wanted to find the imp and rescue my jacket from the little green thief.

"You sure you didn't see him?" I asked.

Tim shook his head. His face suddenly tightened with fear. "You—you didn't *fight* with him—did you?"

I snickered. "Yeah. I fought with him. I ripped off his tail!"

Tim stared at me for a long while. Then his round face went wide with horror. "You—you're kidding, right?" he stammered.

"No way," I replied, still struggling to catch my breath. "I tore off his tail and stuffed it in my locker."

Tim gasped and shrank back. "NO!"

Then, to my surprise, he turned and started to run the other way.

"Stay away from me!" he called back. "Really. Stay away! You're not safe! You made a horrible mistake. You shouldn't have made him angry!"

"Why? What is he going to do to me?" I shouted.

Tim kept running. He didn't answer. He stopped at the end of the hall and glanced back.

"What's he going to do?" I shouted. "Tell me!"

"You're doomed!" Tim called in a trembling voice. "He won't let you get away now. He won't let you survive!"

"Where is your jacket?" Mom asked.

I stepped into the kitchen and dropped my backpack on the floor next to the counter. "I—I've got to change," I said, shivering.

"You're soaking wet," Mom groaned. She squeezed my hair. Water poured down my face. "How could you walk home in the rain without your jacket?"

"It . . . it was stolen," I muttered.

Her mouth dropped open. "What?"

I couldn't hold back. I didn't care about Tonya's warning. I let the whole story out in one long tidal wave of words.

"An imp haunts the school. He took my jacket. He . . . he's an evil creature. He always picks on the new kids. He made my potatoes swarm with bugs. And . . . and . . ."

"You're not making any sense," Mom said. She

felt my forehead. "Do you have a temperature?"

"No, Mom—really," I insisted. "There's an imp, and he—"

"Hey—your father is home," Mom said, gazing out the kitchen window. "Finish your story when he comes in."

Dad burst into the kitchen carrying a large wire cage. He flashed Mom and me a big grin. "It's show-and-tell time," he announced. "Sam, I have a great idea for you. You're going to love this."

He tossed his wet raincoat onto a chair. Then he motioned for Mom and me to come close to the cage.

"How was your first day at Wilton Middle School?" he asked.

"I was just telling Mom," I said. "There's a problem. You see—"

Dad opened the cage door, reached inside, and pulled out a strange-looking rabbit. The rabbit had beautiful black fur, a tiny pink nose, brown eyes, and drooping ears that were a mile long!

Dad held it carefully between his hands. "This is an ebony rabbit," he said softly. "It's very rare. Have you ever seen fur like that?"

"It looks like mink. It would make a beautiful coat!" Mom joked.

Dad is a director of the town zoo. Mom knows that cracking jokes like that makes him crazy. That's why she does it.

"We have only two of these rabbits," Dad said, frowning at her. "They wouldn't make a very big coat."

"Can I pet him?" I asked. Very gently, I rubbed my hand over its soft fur. "Where did you get him, Dad?"

Dad handed the rabbit to me. "The National Zoo sent us a pair of them," he said. "I brought it home for you. I thought you might like to take it to school. You know. Show it off. Impress the other kids."

I petted the rabbit's soft black fur. "Huh? Take it to school? I don't think so."

"Why not?" Dad asked. "Your new teacher will be impressed. The other kids will like it, too. This is a really valuable rabbit."

I rolled my eyes. "You're joking—right? Dad, I'm in sixth grade, not kindergarten."

"Take it to school tomorrow," Dad insisted. "You always have trouble meeting new kids, Sam. Showing off the rabbit will help you."

"I think it's a very nice idea," Mom chimed in.

"No way," I said. I handed the ebony rabbit back to Dad. "I'm not a baby. I can't bring in a bunny for show-and-tell. The kids will think I'm some kind of a geek. Sorry, Dad. But forget about it."

"It's a very rare animal," Dad argued. "It isn't babyish, Sam. You're making a big mistake."

Once Dad got an idea in his head, it was impossible to change his mind. He was as stubborn as me. And neither of us would ever back down.

I let out a sigh. "Listen, Dad, I—I've got a big problem at school."

Petting the rabbit, he frowned at me. "A problem? On the first day?"

"Yes. There's an imp in the school," I said. "An evil creature. And he—"

Dad laughed. "Don't you ever get tired of crazy stories?"

"Sam, you should take the rabbit to school. Definitely," Mom said. "It's better than dreaming up silly stories. And maybe your teacher will give you extra credit in science."

"No way!" I shouted. "No way! No way!" I screamed the words all the way up to my room. "No way! No way! No way!"

Did the ebony rabbit come to school with me the next day?

Three guesses.

And did it turn out to be one of the most horrifying days of my life?

One guess.

"It's called an ebony rabbit," I said. I held the rabbit up high so everyone in class could see it. "Because of its black fur."

"Cool," Tonya muttered from the first row.

"It has such long ears," Mr. Kimpall said. He stood at the side of the room, leaning on a window. "It looks as if it could trip over them!"

"It came from the National Zoo," I explained. "My dad used to work at that zoo before we moved here. And he still has friends there who send him animals."

"Cool," someone said from the back of the room. "Does it taste good?"

Several kids laughed. I could feel myself blushing.

How did I end up showing the rabbit after all my protests?

I didn't bring it to school. My dad did.

Typical Dad. He has to win every argument.

He showed up at the classroom door about fifteen minutes after school started. He asked Mr. Kimpall if he could see me. Then he handed me the cage.

"*Dad—please!*" I growled through gritted teeth. "*Take it back.*"

"Show it to the class. They'll enjoy it," Dad said. He turned and headed away. "Take good care of it," he called. "It's very valuable."

He had a big grin on his face. He was so totally pleased with himself!

I wanted to heave the cage after him. I was furious. But I couldn't make a big scene in front of the whole class.

I was trapped. I had no choice but to show off the rabbit.

"Can you pick it up by the ears?" Simpson asked.

A few kids laughed.

"I don't know," I answered. "I didn't ask my dad. Some rabbits can be picked up that way. But I don't know about this one."

"Can I pet it?" Tonya asked.

Since I was standing right in front of her, I held it out. She rubbed her hand over its back.

"Can I pet it?" another girl asked.

"Me, too?" Simpson asked, jumping to his feet.

"Whoa. Hold your horses," Mr. Kimpall said, hurrying to the front of the room. "If everyone pets it, it won't have much of that beautiful fur left—will it?"

He turned to me. "Nice job, Sam. Thank your dad for bringing in this unusual rabbit so you could share it with us. You'd better put it back in its cage now."

I carried the rabbit to its cage and carefully locked it inside. Then I searched for a good place to keep the cage.

"I hope your dad will let you bring in other interesting animals," Mr. Kimpall said.

"Over my dead body," I muttered.

I spotted an empty bookshelf against the back wall. "Think the rabbit will be safe over there?" I asked Mr. Kimpall. "I promised my dad . . ."

"That should be fine," Mr. Kimpall said. "I'm sure no one in class will disturb it."

I slid the cage onto the shelf. As I started back to my seat, the classroom door swung open.

Tim, the fifth-grader I'd met in the hall after school yesterday, came walking in. He had a note in his chubby hand, which he carried to Mr. Kimpall.

"Hey, Poster, did you see your brother?" Simpson called out. "Back in that cage!"

Several kids laughed.

Tim's face turned bright red.

"Poster's ears are bigger!" a boy shouted.

51

More laughter.

Tim blushed even more. I could see that he didn't like to be teased.

"Since when do rabbits go *oink-oink*?" another boy joked.

"That will be enough!" Mr. Kimpall said sharply. "Not another word."

He opened the note Tim had brought him and read it quickly. Then he turned to me. "Sam, Ms. Simpkin wants to see you in the office."

I swallowed. "The principal? What did I do?"

Some kids laughed.

"The note doesn't say," the teacher replied. "Why don't you go and find out?"

I climbed up from my desk and hurried out of the room. The principal's office was on the second floor near the front of the building.

I glanced at the clock. Nearly lunchtime.

Ms. Simpkin was a friendly-looking middle-aged woman with straight copper-colored hair pulled back in a ponytail. She wore a dark blue sweater over a long denim skirt.

She had been chewing on a pencil, going through a stack of files. She set the pencil down and smiled at me. "Are you Sam?" she asked.

I nodded. I knew I hadn't done anything wrong. But I still felt nervous. "Yes. Sam Waterbury."

"Well, I just wanted to say welcome," she said. She leaned forward and shook my hand. "I didn't get to meet you yesterday. And I like to meet all of my students."

"Oh. Uh . . . thanks," I said. I couldn't think of anything better to say.

She shuffled through some papers. "I need you to sign these student forms. Here." She handed me the pencil she'd been chewing on.

I signed the papers. When I looked up, she was staring hard at me.

"How is it going so far?" she asked.

"Well . . ." Should I tell her about yesterday? Should I tell her about my battle with the imp?

I couldn't decide.

"It's hard to be a new kid here," she said as if reading my mind. "I know it isn't easy, Sam. But—"

"Ms. Simpkin—call for you on line two!" the secretary shouted from the front office.

Ms. Simpkin smiled again and gave me a quick wave. "Good luck," she whispered. Then she picked up the phone.

Good luck?

Did that mean she knew about my problems with the imp?

The buzzer went off for lunch period. Kids streamed out into the hall, laughing and shouting. Three guys pushed past me, racing to be first in line in the lunchroom.

By the time I reached Mr. Kimpall's room, it was

empty. I glanced to the front of the room. The teacher had left, too.

Then I turned to the rabbit cage on the shelf against the back wall.

And felt a stab of horror jolt my body.

"Oh, no!" I cried. "No. Oh, no . . ."

The cage door stood wide open.

The ebony rabbit was gone.

No. No way. It *can't* be! I told myself.

I had closed the cage door so carefully. And I had fastened the latch.

My hands suddenly felt ice cold. My legs wobbled weakly as I stumbled up to the cage.

The rabbit couldn't get out on its own, I decided. No way it could push the door open.

But why would anyone open the cage and let it out?

Unless . . .

No!

The imp wouldn't come into Mr. Kimpall's classroom—would he?

And how would the creature even know that my

55

dad had brought a valuable rabbit to school?

"Where are you, rabbit?" I called out loud, my voice quivering. "Where did you go?"

Panic made my chest flutter. My heart was thudding like a drum.

I checked the windows. All closed.

So the rabbit couldn't have escaped outside.

I dropped to my hands and knees and searched the floor.

No sign of it.

I crawled along the radiator, searching inside the hot air vents.

No. No rabbit.

"Ohhhh." A weak sigh escaped my mouth. I felt sick.

How could I ever explain to my dad?

I climbed to my feet and opened the supply closet door. I clicked on the light and gazed all around for the rabbit.

No. Not in the closet.

When I turned around, I heard footsteps. Mr. Kimpall stepped into the room, carrying a cardboard container of coffee.

"Sam?" He stopped at the doorway. "What are you doing in here? Why aren't you at lunch?"

"The rabbit . . ." I choked out. "It's . . . gone!"

Mr. Kimpall's eyes went to the open cage. His face filled with alarm. "How did it get out? I didn't see anyone go near it."

"The clasp was opened," I said. "I—I've got to find it. My dad will *kill* me!"

Mr. Kimpall glanced around the room. "It couldn't have gone far," he said. "Don't worry, Sam. We'll find it. I'll tell Ms. Simpkin to make an announcement. We'll have the whole school searching."

"I've got to find it *now!*" I shouted. "The rabbit is so valuable. If anything happens—"

He checked his watch. "I have to meet with some parents right now. But it won't take long. I'll be right back, Sam. And then I'll help you search."

He hurried from the room.

I can't just stand here and wait, I thought. I've got to keep searching. I need some help.

I hurried out to the hall. I closed the classroom door behind me in case the rabbit was hiding somewhere in the room.

Then I ran to the lunchroom. I found Tonya just finishing her lunch at a table of girls.

"Quick—you've got to help me!" I cried. I tugged her up from her chair.

"Sam, what's your problem?" she asked.

"The rabbit—it got out."

"Oh, no." She started to follow me out of the lunchroom.

Simpson hurried after us. "Did you say the rabbit escaped?" he asked.

I nodded. "It didn't escape. Someone let it out."

His mouth dropped open. "The imp," he muttered.

I felt a chill of fright at the back of my neck. "No . . ." I muttered.

"My cousin told me you had a fight with the imp yesterday," Simpson said.

I squinted at him. "Your cousin?"

"Yeah, Tim Poster. Did you really tear off the imp's tail?"

Tonya and Simpson both stared hard at me.

"Well . . . yeah. I did," I answered. "But you don't think . . ." My voice trailed off.

"If the imp took the rabbit, you'll never see it again," Simpson said. "That will be the imp's revenge."

"Simpson, don't scare him!" Tonya cried. "First we have to help Sam search, okay?"

"Yeah. Sure," Simpson said. "But the imp always has to have his revenge. That's why you should never fight it. Never give it a hard time. It isn't worth it."

"Stop talking about the imp," Tonya said. "Can't you see Sam is scared to death?"

I led the way back to the classroom. "It might still be in the room," I said. I crossed my fingers on both hands and held them up in front of me.

Tonya patted me on the back. "We'll cover every inch," she promised.

We searched the entire room, up and down. Then we went to the next classroom and searched there.

Kids started coming back to class. Lunch period was nearly over.

I asked if anyone had seen my rabbit. But no one had.

"How did it get out of the cage?" a girl asked me.

"Good question," I replied unhappily.

Still no sign of Mr. Kimpall. I decided I'd better go to the principal's office and ask Ms. Simpkin to make an announcement over the loudspeakers.

"Please keep searching," I told Tonya and Simpson. Then I hurried down the hall.

Halfway to the office, I passed my locker. What was that on the floor in front of it?

I squinted hard, trying to make out what I was seeing.

Did someone leave something there?

Staring hard, I bumped into two little girls carrying some kind of science display. "Watch where you're going!" one of them cried.

"You almost broke it!" the other girl yelled.

"Sorry," I muttered.

I hurried past them. My heart started to pound even harder in my chest. I could barely catch my breath.

What *is* that in front of my locker door?

I stepped up to it and dropped to the floor.

"Nooooooo."

A shrill howl of horror escaped my throat.

I grabbed the sides of my head. And stared down at the little pile . . .

. . . the little pile of bones on the floor.

No. No. No.

The bones had been picked clean. They gleamed as if they had never had any meat on them.

I pictured the ebony rabbit, so soft and pretty.

Then I pictured the green imp, gripping the rabbit between its big hands. Sinking its teeth into the rabbit's belly.

Chewing. Chewing.

Chewing and swallowing the beautiful rabbit chunk by chunk. Then licking the bones clean. Licking them until they shone.

Leaning over the carefully stacked bones, I felt sick.

My stomach lurched. I clamped a hand over my mouth.

I shut my eyes and held my breath, waiting for the tight feeling in my throat to pass.

I pictured my dad.

What could I say to him? How could I explain?

Would he lose his job because of this?

I opened my eyes and forced myself to stand up straight.

Words on my locker door came into focus.

Words scrawled in red paint. A message I had seen before: READ MY LETTER: WHO WILL DROP FIRST?

"I'm not going to take this," I muttered. I clenched my hands into tight fists.

"That ugly green creature won't get away with this."

My hand trembled as I unlocked my locker and pulled open the door. Carefully, I cupped my hands and lifted the pile of bones onto my locker floor.

I picked up the imp's tail. It still felt warm, even though it was no longer attached. I wrapped it like a garden hose and shoved it to the back of the top shelf.

Even if the imp opens my locker again, he's too short to reach it, I thought.

Then I closed the locker and hurried to Ms. Simpkin's office.

Several kids were bunched in front of the counter. I pushed my way into the middle of them and called to the secretary. "I've got to see Ms. Simpkin—right away!"

The secretary, a large, gray-haired woman in a flowery dress, was on the phone. She motioned with one hand for me to wait.

"But it's an emergency!" I shouted. "A valuable rabbit has been eaten and—"

The woman lowered the phone from her ear. "The principal isn't in. She's away at a meeting this afternoon."

"Huh?" I stared at her in disbelief. "This is an emergency!"

She had returned to her phone call. The other kids were staring at me.

I spun away from the counter and ran out of the office. My mind was whirring. I didn't even pay any attention to where I was going.

I shoved open the front doors of the school and leaped outside. I gazed out at a bright, sunny day. A gust of cold wind reminded me it was November.

What am I doing out here? I asked myself.

Where am I going?

Home. That was the answer.

I'm going to tell Mom and Dad. I'm going to tell them the whole story—and this time I'm going to make them believe it.

I'm going to tell them how this whole school lives in terror because of that evil creature.

I stopped at the bottom of the front steps.

Another blast of wind made the flag on the flag-pole snap. The sound—right above me head—made me look up.

I squinted at the flapping flag—and at the dark object at the top of the pole.

Dark object?

What *was* that up there?

"I don't believe it!" I cried.

I realized I was staring up at the ebony rabbit. It was tied to the top of the flagpole.

Was it alive?

I knew I should go into the school. Find the janitors. Have them bring out their ladders.

But I was too excited. Too worried. Too desperate.

"You've got to be alive. You've *got* to!" I shouted up to the rabbit.

Or did the imp kill it first? And then tie it to the flagpole?

With a loud cry, I took a running leap onto the pole. I wrapped my hands around the cold metal. Gripping it tightly, I pressed my sneakers against the pole—and pushed myself up.

Sliding my hands up, I pulled myself higher. My sneakers slipped over the smooth metal pole.

I glanced down. I was nearly halfway up the pole.

With a groan, I forced myself higher. My hands were rubbed raw. I tightened my legs around the pole.

I'm not much of a climber. I've never been into climbing trees. And I'd never shinnied up a flagpole before.

But get me angry enough—and I can do anything.

As I pulled myself higher, I stared up at the rabbit.

I could see one dark eye. The eye was open.

Did that mean the rabbit was alive?

A blast of cold wind made the flagpole sway.

My hand slipped.

I made a frantic grab for the pole, and started to slide back down.

"Noooo!" A cry escaped my throat as I squeezed my legs tighter. And held on for dear life.

I stopped to catch my breath. My hands were cold and raw. My legs ached.

I gazed up at the rabbit, only a few feet above me.

And saw its nose twitch.

Yes!

It's alive, I realized.

The eye stared down at me. I could see its whole body heaving beneath the thick rope. The long ears stood stiffly, straight back.

The poor thing looks scared to death, I thought.

I raised my hand. Gripped the pole. Moved my legs up. Raised my other hand. Pulled myself up.

And touched the rabbit.

"Whoa." Its little heart was beating so hard.

Holding on with one hand, I worked at the rope with the other hand. It slipped off easily and fell to the ground.

The rabbit started to fall, too.

Its ears flew straight up. Its eyes went wide.

I grabbed it and tucked it under my arm.

Then, gripping it tightly in my armpit, I began to lower myself slowly, carefully, down the pole.

In the school windows, I could see crowds of kids and teachers watching me. They stood pressed to the glass, staring as if watching some kind of show.

I saw the secretary from the office and a few teachers come running out of the building.

"What are you doing up there?" the secretary shouted.

"Young man—come down right now!"

"What do you *think* I'm doing?" I shouted down to them.

A few seconds later, my sneakers touched the ground. I dropped to my knees and struggled to catch my breath, to stop my heart from racing so fast.

The teachers huddled around me.

"Are you okay?"

"Are you hurt?"

"What were you doing up there?"

"Your parents will have to be told about this, young man."

I pulled the ebony rabbit from under my arm. Its

fur had been squeezed flat by my tight grip.

"Safe and sound!" I said breathlessly.

And then I saw the square tag tied around its neck. A square tag with some writing on it.

Holding the rabbit gently in one hand, I lifted the tag. And read the message scrawled in red ink: *Have you learned an IMPortant lesson? Give me my tail!*

Tonya and Simpson surrounded me in the hall after school.

I had the rabbit safely in its cage and was about to carry it home. But my two new friends blocked the way.

"Don't tell your parents," Tonya warned. "I know you're angry, but don't tell them about the imp."

I glared at her. "You're kidding—right? Of *course* I'm going to tell them what happened. Someone has to do something about the imp."

Frowning, Simpson grabbed my arm. "There is nothing you can do, Sam."

"He is too powerful," Tonya said.

"I can be powerful, too!" I cried. "Especially when I'm this angry!"

Tonya slapped her hand over my mouth. "Shut up, Sam. What if he hears you?"

I tugged her hand away.

"I don't care!" I shouted. "I don't care if he hears me or not! He's a little creep, and he chose the wrong kid to pick on."

I tried to push past them. But again they moved to block my way.

"Don't you understand?" Simpson said in a whisper. "He has powers. He uses magic. He can do horrible things. Do you know what he did to me?"

I stared at Simpson. "No. What?"

"I was the new kid a few years ago," Simpson said. "The imp wanted to show me who was boss. He made me float off the floor in the art room. He covered me in papier mâché. It was like being buried alive. I had layer after layer of papier mâché all around me. I couldn't move. I couldn't breathe. He hung me out the window like a piñata."

Simpson sighed. "The fire department had to pull me down. Everyone wanted to know how it happened. I . . . I never told. I was too frightened."

"When I was in third grade, there was a boy in my class named Jared Clooney," Tonya said. "Jared was like you, Sam. He tried to fight the imp. One day, the imp made Jared's fingernails and toenails start to grow. They sprouted from his fingers and toes and stretched longer and longer."

"Whoa. Gross," I muttered.

"Jared's nails curled around him," Tonya continued. "They grew so fast. He could only watch in horror. In a minute or so, his nails formed a cage around him. He was trapped inside his own nails!"

"What happened to him?" I asked.

"An ambulance took him away," Tonya replied. "We never saw him again."

"The imp was just teasing you by taking your rabbit," Simpson said. "If he really wanted to hurt you, he could—easily."

"You two are total wimps," I said. "The imp is afraid of *me*! I have his tail! I have him scared!"

But as I walked home carrying the rabbit cage at my side, I wasn't so sure. My stomach felt heavy, knotted. My heart raced. And I couldn't stop picturing a boy trapped inside his own finger- and toe-nails.

Mom and Dad greeted me at the front door with grim faces. "Sam, you're in major trouble," Dad said.

Mom bit her bottom lip. "You promised us things would be different at this school."

Dad took the cage from my hand and led me into the living room. "We just got a call from the school secretary," he said. "She told us about your stunt, climbing the flagpole."

"But—but—" I sputtered.

"The principal is very worried about you," Mom said.

"Why do you have to show off like that?" Dad asked. "It's only your second day of school. Why did you do it, Sam?"

"It wasn't my fault," I replied.

The wrong thing to say.

They lectured me until dinnertime.

I have to do something about the imp, I thought bitterly.

But—what?

That night, I sat down at my computer and went online. I searched the Internet for information about imps.

I stopped at a Web site that showed an artist's drawing of an imp. I stared at the drawing for a long time.

The creature staring back at me looked exactly like the imp at school. It could have been a photograph.

It had light green skin with patches of darker green fur in several places. It had sharp, pointed ears poking up over a fur-thatched head.

And a face with human features—human eyes, nose, lips.

In the drawing, a smile curled up on the imp's face. A cold, thin-lipped smile. An evil smile.

I scrolled down and let my eyes skim over the Web site's information.

It said that imps were creatures of myth and legend. Scientists had no proof that imps had ever existed.

"That's because the scientists didn't come to my school!" I declared.

I scanned the description of the typical imp. Short, two to three feet tall. Sometimes their tails stretched behind them for two to three feet.

It said that imps were playful and mischievous.

They loved games of all kinds, especially word games. They loved disguises, teasing others, practical jokes.

But they hated to be laughed at.

If someone laughed at an imp or ridiculed him, it drove him into a frenzy. It made him furious enough to shrink away forever.

Imps have a strong need to challenge humans, I read. They need to prove that they are smarter than humans, more clever and more powerful.

They have short tempers. Any little thing can make them angry. And once they become angry, they turn vicious.

"Tell me about it," I muttered.

Leaning over my keyboard, I continued to read the information about imps. The next paragraph was a real shocker. I had to read it three times before it really sank in. . . .

Imps have all kinds of magic. Their only limits are

the limits of their imagination.

Perhaps their most powerful magic is the ability to pass as humans. Imps can change their shape in an instant. They can disguise themselves as humans for several hours at a time.

After a while, the strain on their magic becomes too great. And they must go back to their imp bodies to refresh their energy.

"Whoa."

Reading and rereading this section, I suddenly had chills.

Imps can change shape and disguise themselves as humans. Humans . . .

My brain was spinning.

I had to shut off the computer.

Then I flopped onto my bed. I closed my eyes, thinking hard.

Was the imp disguising himself as someone at my new school?

Is that how he hid all day from everyone? Is that how he spied on the kids?

Is that how he knew my dad had brought the ebony rabbit to school yesterday?

Was it someone I knew?

One of the teachers? One of the kids?

One of my new friends?

At school the next morning, I looked at everyone differently. As I walked to my classroom, I studied the kids who passed by me.

Was one of them the imp?

I stepped into the room and waved hello to Mr. Kimpall. Was he the imp? I wondered.

He is nearly as short as the imp! I thought. But he's too nice to be the disgusting creature, I decided.

We had a geography test that morning. But I couldn't concentrate on it.

I kept gazing around the room, staring at the other kids as they filled in their test papers. Was one of them the imp?

I watched Tonya. She leaned over her paper,

moving her lips as she wrote. Tonya was left-handed, I saw.

Were imps left-handed? Was that a clue?

I turned and watched Simpson. He kept scratching his spiky brown hair with his pencil. He shook his head, frowning down at the test questions.

Simpson always seems terrified of the imp, I thought. And I am pretty sure he's not pretending to be afraid.

Of course, I could be wrong. Simpson could be the imp.

All of this thinking was making my head spin. And I realized if I didn't get down to work, I was going to flunk the test.

It's no good to suspect everyone, I told myself. That won't get me anywhere.

I need clues.

Of course, the scrawled messages from the imp were clues.

"READ MY LETTER: WHO WILL DROP FIRST?" That had to be some kind of clue.

The Web site said that imps love to play games, especially word games. They love to challenge humans.

Was that message some kind of word game? What could it mean?

"Time is up," Mr. Kimpall said from the front of the room. "Put down your pencils."

"Oh, no," I muttered. I gazed down at my test paper. I hadn't written a word.

I really tried. But I couldn't get the imp out of my mind.

That afternoon, I stepped into the band room for rehearsal and gazed around. I saw Teri changing her clarinet reed.

She could be the imp, I thought.

Or Mr. Kelly. Or the big kid who plays the tuba.

Ms. Simpkin poked her head into the room and waved hello to Mr. Kelly.

She could be the imp, I thought.

What if the principal of the school was the imp? Would that explain why all the teachers were so terrified?

My head throbbed. I realized I was gritting my teeth.

Sam, you've got to relax, I told myself. You are totally stressed.

Maybe practicing on my sax will help calm me down, I thought. Playing music usually helped.

I pulled my sax case off the shelf. I dropped to my knees and started to open it—and saw a white sheet of paper taped to the top.

"Whoa. What's this?" I muttered.

I tugged the paper off the case. And stared at the red letters, scrawled in paint: READ MY LETTER:

WHO WILL DROP FIRST?

"Oh, wow." A voice behind me made me spin around.

I found Teri standing there, reading the note over my shoulder. "Sam—be careful," she said softly.

I let the note fall to the floor. "I'm not afraid of stupid notes that don't even make any sense!" I cried angrily.

I grabbed the sax case and pulled it open. Then I lifted out the two sections of the horn.

I started to slide them together. Then stopped.

Wait. Something felt funny. Something was wrong.

I tried to set the sax sections back in the case. But my hands wouldn't let go.

My fingers were wrapped tightly around them. I tried to raise my fingers. To uncurl them.

But they were stuck tightly to the saxophone pieces.

"Hey!" I cried.

I shook my hands hard. But they wouldn't come unstuck.

My heart pounding, I stared at the two sax sections. Someone had poured a thick layer of glue over them.

No matter how I moved, I couldn't pull my hands away.

"Mr. Kelly? I need help here!" I shouted. My

voice came out high and shrill.

Several kids turned to stare at me.

Mr. Kelly had been talking to the snare drummers. He turned, saw me down on the floor beside my sax case, and hurried over.

"Sam, what's the problem?"

I raised my hands with the horn sections attached. "I'm stuck," I said. "My hands are glued to the sax."

Mr. Kelly's mouth dropped open in shock. He bent down beside me. He gave one of the sax parts a gentle tug.

"See?" I said. "I'm totally stuck."

He stared at my hands. "Let's see what we can do," he muttered.

He grabbed the fingers on my left hand and tried to pry them up.

No. They wouldn't budge.

He grabbed the sax section and pulled with all his strength.

I heard a ripping sound—and felt a wave of pain sweep down my arm.

"OW! NO—STOP!" I screamed. "MY SKIN! MY SKIN IS TEARING OFF!"

Mr. Kelly phoned my parents. He said they would meet me at the emergency room.

He helped me to my feet, then guided me to his car in the teacher parking lot. Kids stared at me as I made my way through the hall.

Some kids thought it was a joke. But they stopped laughing when they saw the pain on my face. I heard some kids murmuring about the imp.

Mr. Kelly held open the door to his gray Camry. I lowered myself into the seat and rested the sax parts in my lap.

"The doctors will know how to unstick them," he said. He was trying to sound cheerful. But I could tell by his voice that he was really worried.

As we pulled into the hospital parking lot, Mr. Kelly turned to me. He stared down at the sax pieces, then raised his eyes to me.

"Don't tell your parents about the imp," he said softly.

My mouth felt dry as dust. I swallowed. "Excuse me?"

"If he finds out about it, it will only make things worse," Mr. Kelly said.

I groaned and tried to raise my hands. "How could things be any worse?" I asked.

"If the secret gets out, the imp will go berserk," Mr. Kelly said. "He will hurt people. He really will. He will go after everyone in the school."

I saw my parents crossing the parking lot. Dad held Mom's arm. They looked really worried.

"There they are," I told Mr. Kelly. I pointed.

He grabbed my sleeve. "Don't tell, Sam," he repeated. "I'm warning you."

We caught up to my parents at the front desk. They turned and stared in shock at the pieces of the saxophone stuck to my hands.

Before I could open my mouth, Mr. Kelly spoke up. "Someone at school played a cruel trick," he told them. "The principal is looking into it."

Dr. Gubbin didn't know what to do. He was a young man with a short black ponytail hanging from the back of his green surgical cap.

He had me perched in front of him on a metal exam table. He kept rubbing the front of his green gown with both hands, studying my hands. Studying me as if I were an alien from a different planet.

He tsk-tsked several times and kept shaking his head. Then he tried rubbing a few different liquids over my hands.

They were supposed to loosen the glue. But they didn't work.

My hands were totally cramped now. And my shoulders ached from holding the heavy metal sax parts for so long.

Finally, he turned to my parents. They were huddled together on the other side of the exam table.

"I may have to try a mild acid," he said.

"NO WAY!" I shouted.

"If I can't find something to dissolve the glue, I might have to burn it off," Dr. Gubbin said. "It will do some skin damage. But we should be able to heal it up in a month or so."

"Please—" I begged. "No acid!"

Dad's face had turned as green as the doctor's lab gown. "If that's the only way . . ." he muttered.

"It will burn a little bit," Dr. Gubbin told me.

"No. Please—" I repeated. "If you burn my hands . . ."

I tried to raise them—and one hand pulled loose.

The saxophone piece clattered to the floor.

"Hey—!"

Everyone cried out at once.

"See?" I said. "We don't need acid!"

"Good news. I guess that last solvent did the trick," Dr. Gubbin said. "Let's apply some more to the other hand and see what happens."

A few minutes later, Dr. Gubbin released my other hand.

A few minutes after that, I was riding home with my parents in the backseat of the Taurus. My hands still stung and ached. Patches of skin had been torn off on both palms, and two of my fingers had to be bandaged.

"Sam, who would do such a horrible thing to you?" Mom asked, turning to face me from the passenger seat.

"You just started this school," Dad said, turning onto Palm Street. "You haven't made any enemies already—have you?"

"Well . . ."

I took a deep breath and let it all come out.

"I told you, but you wouldn't listen to me. The school is haunted by a vicious creature," I said. "He's about three feet tall and looks like a big green rat. Except he has a human face."

"Excuse me?" Mom turned around again to look at me.

"It's an imp," I continued. "Imps are not supposed to be real. But this one is."

I took another breath. The words came tumbling out of me. "Everyone in school is terrified of the imp," I said. "Even the teachers. The imp has magical powers, and he can do horrible things if he gets angry.

"Remember when I came home without my jacket?" I continued breathlessly. "I told you the imp took it. You laughed at me. But it was true. I tried to take back the jacket. I got into a fight with him. And I pulled off his tail."

I raised my raw red hands. "This was his revenge," I said. "A kid didn't do this to me. The imp did."

We weren't home yet. But Dad pulled the car to the curb. He and Mom both turned to me. "Sam—" Dad started.

"You've got to help me," I said. "We've got to get rid of this imp. No one else will do it. So, will you help me? Will you?"

My parents stared at me for the longest time. Mom chewed her bottom lip. Dad tapped his fingers nervously on the seat back.

"You believe me—don't you?" My question came out in a whisper.

Mom shook her head.

"Sam, this is exactly what you did at your last school," Dad said. "Blaming your problems on others."

"You promised us you wouldn't do this anymore," Mom said in a trembling voice. "You are making up stories to keep from facing the truth."

"But this time you've gone too far. Your story is too crazy for *anyone* to believe," Dad said.

"I'm very worried about you," Mom said. "Very worried."

"Me too," Dad said softly.

"You . . . don't believe me," I muttered. I had a heavy lump in my throat.

I wanted them to believe me. I *needed* them to believe me.

"Okay. I'll prove it to you," I said.

I knew what I had to do. I had to draw the imp out. I had to force a showdown.

The next morning, I hurried to the computer room before school started. I printed up a bunch of signs. The signs read "READ *MY* LETTER: *YOU* WILL DROP FIRST!"

I took a roll of tape from the art room, and I began taping up my signs all over school.

"Sam, are you crazy?" a voice called.

I turned to find Tonya staring at me in horror. She wore a stiff-looking white blouse and a black skirt over black tights.

I finished taping a sign to the science lab door. "Why are you dressed like a pilgrim? It's not Thanksgiving," I said.

"I'm in the chorus," she replied, staring at the sign. "We're singing at the assembly this morning."

"Oh, yeah," I muttered. I had forgotten there was an assembly.

Good, I thought. Good timing.

"Take that sign down, Sam," Tonya warned. "What do you think you're doing?"

"It's war," I said. "Me against the imp. No way I'm taking it down."

I held up my stack of signs. "Help me put them up?"

She brushed back her straight black hair. "You're crazy," she said. "How can you be so crazy after what the imp did to you yesterday?"

I began walking down the hall, searching for a good place to hang the next sign. "Don't you want to get rid of the imp, Tonya?" I asked. "Don't you want to go to a normal school where people aren't afraid all the time?"

"Of course," she replied, following after me. "But there's no way. He has too much power, Sam. Your signs are only going to make him angry. And when he's angry—"

I grabbed Tonya's arm. "I'm angry, too," I said. "Look what he did to my hands." I showed her the cuts and burns. "I'm angry, too, Tonya. That's why I'm going to do everything I can to get rid of the creature."

She tried to pull free. But I held on to her arm. "Why won't you help me, Tonya? Why?"

We both jumped as Ms. Simpkin came around the corner. "Sam? Tonya?" The principal hurried over to us.

"Tonya, the chorus is already onstage," she said. "You'd better get over there."

She turned to me. "Sam, why aren't you in class? The assembly will be starting in a few minutes."

"I—I have these signs," I said. I started to hold them up.

But Ms. Simpkin spun away and trotted back the other way. "Let's go, you two," she called back to us. "We have a guest speaker this morning. We don't want to hold up the assembly."

Tonya turned and ran toward the auditorium.

I stared after her, thinking hard. An assembly . . . An assembly . . .

Suddenly, I had a plan.

The assembly was pretty boring. But no one cared. It meant we got out of class.

The chorus sang two songs. They sounded pretty good. But the girl at the end of the top row slipped during the first song and nearly fell off the bleacher.

She caught her balance. But her face stayed bright red for the rest of the performance.

The speaker was a young woman who talked about volunteering to help out with things in the community. She said kids could make a real difference, and it wouldn't take up much of our time.

I didn't really hear too much of her talk. I could only think about the imp and what I planned to do.

Yes, you're right. I was obsessed.

I had made up my mind to destroy the imp once and for all. And nothing was going to stop me.

When the speaker finished, most kids clapped. A few kids in the back rows booed, just to be funny.

Ms. Simpkin glared at them. Then she walked to the podium to thank the speaker.

I took a deep breath and jumped up from my seat. I pushed my way over kids' legs to the aisle.

"Hey, Sam—where are you going?"

"Sam, sit down!"

"Ow! Get off my foot!"

I ignored the kids in my row who tried to stop me. I knew what I was going to do. I had been planning it all through the assembly.

Ms. Simpkin didn't see me run down the aisle. She didn't see me climb onto the stage.

She was making an announcement about the band concert on Friday night. "I want everyone here to cheer on our great band," she said.

I don't think she noticed me until I was standing next to her at the podium.

She let out a startled cry as I pulled the microphone from her hand.

I moved away from her and turned to the audience. "Hey, imp—!" I shouted into the microphone. "Hey, imp—you want me? Come find me!"

My hands were trembling. My voice came out high and shrill.

But I didn't care.

I lifted the microphone close to my mouth. "Come find me!" I screamed.

And then I held up the imp's tail. I raised it high over my head in my free hand. And I waved it in the air.

"You want this back?" I screamed. "Hey, imp—you want this back? Come and get it! I dare you! Come and *try* to get it back!"

I shook the limp green tail, waving it high over my head. "YOU will drop first!" I cried. "Come and get this! Come on—unless you're chicken!"

I stopped to take a breath. My heart was pounding. My whole body was trembling.

Were the kids cheering me on? Were they behind me?

No.

A heavy silence had fallen over the auditorium.

I saw pale faces staring up at me in wide-eyed horror.

I sank back. I lowered the tail to my side.

Have I gone too far? I wondered.

Have I?

The answer was *yes*.

The next day, the imp went berserk.

I was tense the rest of the day.

Every sound made me jump. Every loud voice sent a chill of fear down my back.

Would the imp come after me?

Was he waiting for me around the next corner? Outside the classroom? Behind the school?

I could see that the other kids were frightened, too.

No one spoke to me. In the lunchroom, kids stayed as far away from me as possible.

I sat at a table in the back all by myself. The lunchroom was a lot quieter than normal. Kids spoke in whispers, glancing at me, then turning away.

"What's the matter?" I shouted. "Is everyone too chicken to help me?"

No one answered.

I couldn't eat my lunch. My mouth was dry as sand. My stomach felt all fluttery.

As I walked back to my classroom, I realized a hush had fallen over the entire school. A terrified hush.

Everyone was waiting . . . waiting for the imp to take his revenge on me.

I guess I'm on my own, I thought.

I guess I'm the only kid in this school brave enough to stand up to that creature.

The next afternoon, I suddenly wasn't feeling so brave.

We had been working hard all day. And we'd had a really long spelling test. So Mr. Kimpall gave us a free half hour to do whatever we wanted.

I walked over to Simpson and Tonya, who were passing a Game Boy back and forth.

"I need to talk to you two," I said softly. "I really think you should help me. I—"

"No way," Simpson replied sharply. "Go away, Sam—please."

"Stay away from us," Tonya said.

I could see they weren't trying to be mean. They were *frightened*.

"If the imp heard what you said yesterday afternoon," Tonya whispered. "We could all be in major trouble."

And that's when things went crazy.

I felt a spray of something cold on my head. Then my shoulders.

Cold water!

Kids started to scream. Chairs scraped.

I gazed up—and saw that the ceiling sprinklers were gushing water.

"Whoa!" In a few seconds, I was drenched.

Kids were screaming, running to the door.

Water splashed over the desks, puddling rapidly over the linoleum floor.

Mr. Kimpall was scrambling around his desk, frantically trying to rescue his books and papers.

I took a few running steps—and slipped in a deep puddle of water.

My feet slid out from under me. I landed hard on my back.

And that's when I heard the popping sound.

At first, I thought it was popcorn popping.

But then I saw a ceiling light pop and shatter.

Then another. Another.

A whole row of lights exploded.

Jagged shards of glass rained down over the room.

Covering my head, I scrambled to my feet.

My shoes slid over broken glass.

POP! POP!

Two more big bulbs exploded. The pieces of glass

sparkled as they fell through the spray of sprinkler water.

Most kids had made it safely out of the room. I could still hear their screams from out in the hall.

Mr. Kimpall had a pile of books under his arms. Ducking the falling glass, he slipped and slid to the door.

"Sam—hurry!" he called, waving frantically to me.

A hard burst of water splashed down on me. I felt a sharp stab of pain as a piece of an exploded light-bulb grazed the shoulder of my drenched T-shirt.

Lowering my head, I struggled toward the door.

I was nearly there, when I heard the buzzing crackle of electricity.

Looking up, I saw a bright yellow-white bolt shoot across the ceiling.

Red and yellow sparks flew everywhere.

ZZZZAAAAPPPPP.

A jagged bolt of electricity hit the wall in front of me. It bounced off, sending a shower of sparks over the wet floor.

Ducking my head, I heard another explosion of glass. And then another bolt of electricity flashed above me.

Gasping for breath, I stumbled to the classroom door.

I grabbed the metal doorknob.

And opened my mouth in a scream of agony as a powerful jolt of electricity burned through my hand . . . rattled my teeth . . . shot through my body.

My hand—I couldn't remove it from the doorknob.

Shock after shock made my whole body jump and twist.

Dancing . . . dancing out of control in the white-hot jolts of electricity, I knew the imp had had his victory.

My battle had ended before it had even begun.

ZZZZZZZZTTTT.

A body-shattering bolt of power shot me to the floor in a crumpled heap.

I tried to climb to my feet. But I couldn't make my muscles work.

Gasping, throbbing in pain, I lay flopping on the wet floor like a dying fish.

"Unnnnh." A sick groan escaped my open mouth.

I saw bright flashes of red and yellow dancing around me.

Then I felt strong arms pulling me, sliding me over the wet floor.

I blinked several times. I let out a strong whoosh of air, forcing myself to start breathing again.

I looked up to see who had rescued me. "Teri?"

She let go of my arms. And sank back into the crowd that had formed a circle around me.

I gazed up at Mr. Kimpall, Simpson, and Tim Poster.

"Sam? Can you hear me? Can you speak?" Mr. Kimpall asked, lowering his face to mine.

"Uh . . ." I struggled to answer. My face wasn't working right. I couldn't get my lips to form words.

"You had a nasty shock," Mr. Kimpall said. "Lie still. We called for a doctor to come check you out."

Tim and Simpson stared down at me as if I were some sort of alien creature. Behind them I saw the other kids from my class, all soaked, shaking from the cold.

"I don't know what set the sprinklers off," Mr. Kimpall said, still leaning over me. "I've never seen anything like that."

I know what set them off, I thought bitterly. *His name is spelled i-m-p.*

And all that destruction, all that horror had only one target—

Me.

The doctor arrived a few minutes later. She examined me carefully and said I was okay.

Ms. Simpkin offered to drive me home. On the way, she lectured me about the big mistake I'd made at the assembly.

"The whole school had to pay for your little outburst," she said sternly. "But you were lucky this time, Sam. The imp let you survive."

She turned to me as she parked in front of my house. "The next time . . ." she said. "The next time . . ." Her voice trailed off.

I felt a shiver of fear.

I had felt so brave before. So sure of myself.

But I had seen the power of the imp. Thinking about it sent chill after chill down my back.

"Don't you want to get rid of the imp?" I asked Ms. Simpkin. "Don't you want to chase it away so the school can be normal?"

She didn't answer. Instead, she waved me out of the car. "See you tomorrow, Sam," she said softly. "I hope."

Friday afternoon, we had a long band practice after school. Our last chance to work on our songs before the concert that night.

I sat down next to Teri and started to warm up. "How's it going?" I asked her. "You nervous about tonight? Are your parents coming?"

My parents were coming to the concert tonight straight from work.

Teri didn't answer. She moved her music stand so that she could turn her back to me. She started playing scales on her clarinet really loud.

"Okay, okay. I can take a hint," I said. I grabbed her shoulder and forced her to stop playing.

"The imp isn't going to hurt you just because you

talk to me," I said. "I'm the one who challenged the imp—not you. I'm the one who's in trouble."

"Sam, you don't know what you're saying," she said. She kept her back to me. "Look at all the trouble you've caused. No one feels safe now. Why did you have to stir things up?"

"I . . . I just want things to be normal," I said. "I don't see why everyone in this school—"

"The imp is going to do something horrible at the concert tonight," Teri said. "I know he is. And it will be all your fault."

"But if we all join together—" I started to say. "If we find out who it is and stand up to him . . ."

She raised her clarinet to her mouth and began playing scales again.

I let out a sigh. Then I started to warm up again.

Usually, playing my saxophone relaxes me. But not today. I had a tight knot in my throat. I could barely blow hard enough to make a sound.

"As you know, the concert begins at eight o'clock," Mr. Kelly said at the end of practice. "But you should all be here by seven-thirty."

I glanced at the clock. It was a quarter to five. Not much time.

I had to hurry home, grab some dinner, and change. Mom said she'd leave food for me to warm up in the microwave.

In a way, I was glad Mom and Dad weren't going

to be home. Things had been a little tense at my house ever since I told them about the imp.

My parents kept watching me all the time, as if trying to decide if I had totally lost it or not.

"Good luck tonight," Mr. Kelly said. He glanced at me as he said it. "Have a good concert, people."

Everyone started to pack up. I stayed in my chair, holding on to my sax as if holding on to a life preserver.

I made no attempt to move as Mr. Kelly walked over to me. His eyes locked on mine. "Sam? Are you going to be okay?" he asked softly.

I shrugged. "I guess," I said.

He cleared his throat. He glanced tensely at the band room door. "If you think you should stay home tonight, I'll understand," he said.

I let out an angry cry. "You're afraid, too?" I screamed. "Well, forget about me staying home. I'll be here at seven-thirty sharp."

His mouth dropped open in surprise.

I stomped out of the room without even putting away my horn. My hands were clenched into tight fists. I could feel the anger making my face grow hot.

I made my way down the stairs two at a time.

I hurried down the hall. Turned the corner—and saw the imp standing in front of my locker.

A cold smile spread over his face as he saw me.

He uncurled his back until he stood straight up,

all three feet of him. He pressed his hands against his furry waist, tapping his long, snakelike fingers against his sides.

He kept his gaze on me and took a step toward me. Then another.

I took a deep breath. And held it.

This is it, I realized.

Showdown time.

My legs started to shake.

I struggled to breathe. Raising my fists, I prepared for a fight.

But to my surprise, the imp stopped halfway toward me.

His smile faded. His dark eyes burned into mine.

Slowly, he raised his right hand. And pointed a long, bony finger at me.

He just stood there, glaring at me. His finger pointed at my throat.

We stood frozen like that for a long, long time.

And then the ratlike creature opened his mouth and whispered one word: "*Later.*"

He spun away—and started to run. His bare feet

made loud slapping noises on the hard floor. His body bounced heavily over his slender, running legs.

"Oh." A soft cry of surprise escaped my throat.

And then I took off after him.

"You—you're not getting away!" I tried to shout. But my voice came out in a muffled whisper.

He whipped around the corner, a flash of green.

Gasping for breath, I raced after him.

The school was deserted. The only sounds were the rapid, sharp slap of his bare feet on the floor and my wheezing breaths.

"Help me! Can anyone help me?" I shouted.

My shrill cry rang out through the hall. But there was no one there to reply.

We rounded another corner. And then I saw him flying up the back stairs.

The hall was darker there. The classroom doors were all shut. I realized I had never been in this back hall.

I followed the imp up the stairs. His bouncing body was a dim ball of green against the darkness.

I stopped at the top of the stairs and squinted down the long hall. The ceiling was low. The hall cluttered with stacks of cartons, piles of old books.

The rooms were all empty and dark.

I heard the slap of the imp's feet up ahead. But I couldn't see him.

I forced myself to move.

Stumbling over a box of file folders, I lurched after the creature.

I heard a door slam hard.

I turned and found myself in a narrow, short hallway. I saw only two doors against the wall. Two solid black doors.

I stepped up between them.

The imp had to go into one of these rooms, I knew.

But which one?

Had I followed the imp to his home?

My eyes moved from one door to the other.

Which one? Which one?

Finally, I grabbed the handle of the door on the left—and pulled open the door.

"Tim!" I cried.

Tim Poster was curled up in a black desk chair against the back wall of the small room. As I burst into the room, he dropped the book he had been holding and jumped to his feet.

"Sam—?" he called out, blinking in surprise.

The room was some kind of supply closet. Old computers were stacked in front of the window. Several folding chairs and two desks were pushed against one wall.

A single lamp behind Tim's desk chair provided the only light.

"Tim—it's *you*—isn't it!" I cried. "I—I followed you here! And you—"

His face twisted in confusion. "Huh? What's

106

wrong? What are you talking about?"

He bent to pick up the book he had dropped.

"Tim—I saw you run in here," I said breathlessly. My whole body shook with fear—and excitement. "I—I know your secret."

"Don't tell," he said. He slumped into the desk chair. "Okay, Sam?"

"Don't tell?" I repeated.

"Please don't tell," Tim begged. "I hide up here to read and do my homework after school every day."

"But—but—" I sputtered. This wasn't making any sense.

"I can explain," Tim said. "You see, my house is too noisy and crowded. And my dad thinks I'm on the soccer team. I don't have the nerve to tell him that I never even tried out."

My mouth dropped open. "Your dad thinks you're at soccer practice?"

He nodded. "I found this room," he said. "It's just for storage. No one ever comes up here. So I come here after school."

"You . . . you hide up here?" I asked. My heartbeat was starting to slow to normal.

Tim nodded again. "I do my homework. Then I read. I love to read. I never have a chance at home."

I stared hard at him, studying his face.

He was lying. He had to be lying.

I had chased him up here. He was the imp. I

107

knew he was. There was no other explanation!

He had slammed the door behind him. Changed into his human form. Picked up the book and waited for me to arrive.

"You're the imp, Tim," I said. "I'm not falling for your dumb story. You're the imp, and I've caught you."

He set down the book and climbed slowly to his feet. "No way, Sam," he said softly. "I'm not the imp. I'm just me."

"You were doing something at my locker. I chased you up here," I insisted. "I heard you slam the door."

Tim shook his head. "No. It wasn't me. I heard a door slam, too. But it wasn't this door, Sam. I've been reading up here ever since school let out. Really."

I continued to stare at him. Should I believe him?

"I'll help you find him," Tim said softly. "If you don't tell anyone about my secret hiding place. If you promise not to tell, I'll help you search for him, Sam."

"I opened the wrong door," I muttered. "He must have run into the room next door."

Tim suddenly looked very frightened. "The imp? He's next door? Why would he come up here? No one ever comes up here."

I didn't reply. I spun away from him and ran out of the room.

I grabbed the handle to the door on the right and pulled it open.

Was the imp still in there?

No. I stared into a bare room. No furniture of any kind. A totally empty room. Gray light washed in through the dust-caked windows.

"Where did he go?" I muttered.

Was Tim lying? Was Tim really the imp?

But he seemed so surprised to see me. So desperate to keep his hiding place a secret.

My head spinning, I left Tim and made my way back down the hall. I turned a corner and found myself in a familiar hallway.

The band room stood at the end of this hall. I suddenly remembered that I had hurried out without putting my sax in its case.

I glanced at the clock on the wall. Nearly five-fifteen.

It's really getting late, I realized.

I stepped up to the band room—and stopped in the doorway.

There he was again—the imp!

He had his back to me. He held my saxophone in his hands.

What was he doing to it?

I stopped myself from crying out.

I gazed in horror as the creature raised the horn to his lips. The sax was nearly as tall as he was! He blew into the horn and made a flat noise, more like a burp than a musical note.

Yuck, I thought.

That *creature* has my horn in his mouth!

What does he plan to do to my new sax? Does he plan to ruin it? Is he going to make it explode when I start to play it later? Or make it stick to me again?

My horror quickly turned to anger.

The imp had no right—no right to be ruining my life this way!

My heart pounded. As my anger rose, I could feel the blood pulsing at my temples.

I crept into the room.

The imp still had his back turned. He didn't see me. He blew another sour note on the horn.

Before he could turn around, I ran up behind him.

I made a flying leap.

I wrapped my arms around his waist—and tightened them. Tighter. Tighter.

The sax fell out of his hands and slid to the floor.

He opened his mouth in a shrill, raspy shriek.

He squirmed and twisted hard.

But I held on.

Digging my chin into his back, I tightened my grip around his waist. And held on.

He ducked and tossed. He shrieked again.

His skin felt wet and soft. Slippery.

But I held on. Squeezing him. Squeezing him until he made a gasping, choking sound.

His body went limp. His head slumped forward.

"Gotcha!" I screamed. "I've gotcha!"

He let out one more grunt.

Then his eyes slowly lowered and shut. His head bounced on his chest. All the air seemed to go out of his body, like a balloon deflating.

Was it a trick?

Had I *killed* him?

No. I could feel him breathing.

But his arms and legs dangled as if they had no bones.

I've got him, I thought. Now what do I do with him?

I stumbled to the door.

If only someone were still in the school. Someone who could help me.

I needed to put him somewhere safe, I knew. Somewhere he couldn't escape.

Everyone would be back here in a few hours.

I thought of how shocked everyone would be when they saw that I had captured the imp. Shocked—and thrilled!

But in the meantime, I needed something to keep him in.

The imp uttered a weak groan. His arms twitched.

Was he coming back to life?

Holding him tightly in front of me, I turned back to the band room.

And had an idea.

The imp twitched again. He snapped his head back. His eyelids opened, and I could see his dark eyes rolling in his head.

I knew I had only seconds before he came to life again.

I kicked open my saxophone case. Bent quickly. Lowered the imp into the case.

One spindly green leg dangled over the side. I tucked it in. Slammed the case shut. And with trembling hands fastened the clasps.

"Gotcha," I muttered again.

I felt so dizzy, I had to sit down. I dropped beside the sax case and struggled to catch my breath.

The floor tilted up in front of me. I shut my eyes tight and waited for the dizziness to pass.

I've done it! I told myself happily.

I've captured the imp! In a few hours, everyone will know what I've done!

I could hear the imp banging inside the case. He gave the case several hard thumps. But the metal clasps held.

No way he could pop open the lid.

When I opened my eyes, my gaze fell on a white slip of paper attached to the case.

It took me a few seconds to realize it was the imp's note from the day before.

READ MY LETTER: WHO WILL DROP FIRST?

From inside the case, the imp gave the lid another hard thump.

I stared at the note. Stared at the words one by one.

In my excitement, my brain jumped from thought to thought.

I remembered what I had read about imps. I remembered how they like games and tricks. How they like wordplay.

Wordplay.

READ MY LETTER.

LETTER. DROP FIRST.

The imp thumped against the case again, trying hard to escape.

But I ignored him as these thoughts flew through my mind.

The imp's messages had been a game, I decided. A trick.

The imp wanted everyone to guess. He wanted everyone to figure out who he was.

I stared hard at the scrawled letters on the note.

MY LETTER. DROP FIRST.

DROP MY FIRST LETTER.

And suddenly, I had the answer. It all made sense.

I knew. I *knew*!

I turned to the saxophone case. I gripped it with both hands.

"I know who you are!" I shouted.

The imp stopped banging on the case. A heavy silence fell over the room.

"I figured out your little word game," I said. "I know who you are."

The imp remained quiet.

I shook the case. "Hey, did you hear me?" I called. "I won! I beat you!"

Still no sound from inside the case. Had I suffocated him? Should I risk opening the lid to see if he was okay?

I grabbed the clasps on the sax case and flipped them up. My hands trembling, I raised the lid and gazed down at the small green creature. He had pressed himself into the folds of the case. He stared up at me with wet black eyes and didn't move.

I reached down and wrapped my hands around his narrow waist. Then I lifted him out of the case.

"Simpson, I know it's you," I said. "So snap out of it. Playing dead isn't going to help you."

He blinked. And ran a pointed purple tongue over his green lips. "Put me down," he whispered.

I continued to hold him in front of me. "If I put you down, you won't run away?"

He shook his head. His shoulders slumped. He gazed at me sadly with those wet black eyes. "I can't run away. You have defeated me. By guessing my identity, you have taken away my powers."

I set him down on the floor. He stretched his skinny arms above his head. Then he let out a long, sad sigh.

"Oh—!" I cried out as he began to grow.

His body inflated like a balloon. His bones made loud cracking noises as he changed into a human.

Into Simpson.

Simpson, fully dressed in jeans and a red T-shirt.

"How did you know it was me?" he asked in a muffled whisper.

I moved between him and the door in case he planned to try an escape. I kept my muscles tensed.

No way I would let him get away.

"I figured out your word game," I replied. "The word *imp*—it's hidden right in your name. Drop the first letter. Drop the first letter of Simpson—and you get *impson*. Imp is the hidden word."

He narrowed his eyes at me. "You're smarter than I thought," he muttered. He sighed again. "I had a good thing going here, but now it's over."

He shook his head. "Imps have to play word games. We have to tease humans with them. It's our nature. But I never thought anyone would guess . . ."

"I'm going to tell everyone," I said. "Your days of terrifying the school are over."

"I know," he said, shaking his head again. "You've defeated me, Sam." He shrugged. "I'm finished here."

He gazed at me with a pleading expression. "Can we make a deal?" he asked.

I tensed, studying him. "What kind of deal?"

"Can we make a trade?" he asked softly. "I'll give you back your jacket if you give me my tail."

"I don't know," I replied. "Why should I trust you? It might be some kind of a trick."

He raised his right hand as if swearing an oath. "No tricks. You give me my tail, Sam. I return your jacket. Then I promise I'll go away, and no one at this school will ever see me again."

I squinted hard at him. "You'll go away before the band concert? And you'll never come back to this school?"

He raised his right hand again. "Promise."

I kept staring at him. Had I really defeated him? Had I really freed the school from his terror?

What did the article online say? Did it say what would happen if you guessed an imp's real identity? Did it say that guessing his identity would take away all his powers? I couldn't remember.

"Is it a deal?" he asked eagerly. "Have we got a deal?" He reached out his right hand for me to shake.

I stared hard at him, studying his sad, defeated face.

Could I trust him?

Could I?

Yes, I decided. I shook his hand.

"Go get my tail," Simpson said. "I'll bring your jacket. We'll meet back here in two minutes—okay?"

I hoped I wasn't making a big mistake. "You won't run away and hide?" I asked. "You won't go back to your old tricks at the concert tonight?"

He shook his head. "I can't go back to my old tricks, Sam. You've defeated me."

He seemed so sad and sincere. I had to believe him.

I turned and ran out of the band room. I made my way downstairs and hurried to my locker.

I heard voices down the hall. I saw people heading to the auditorium. The audience had started to arrive for the concert.

I saw two teachers go through the auditorium doors. A couple of kids followed them.

I wanted to run up to them all. I wanted to scream at the top of my lungs: "I did it! I defeated the imp!"

I grabbed the green tail from my locker shelf. I wrapped it around my hand and slammed the locker door shut.

I was running up the steps, on my way back to the band room, when I saw a familiar figure heading down toward me.

"Hey, Tim," I called.

Tim stopped. He lowered his eyes to the tail wrapped around my hand.

"Are you still here? Are you going to the concert?" I asked.

He kept his gaze on the tail. "What are you going to do with that?" he asked.

I hesitated.

Should I tell him?

Yes. I couldn't keep my news to myself any longer. I had to tell someone!

"I did it, Tim!" I exclaimed. "I captured the imp. I captured him, and I figured out who he is!"

Tim's mouth dropped open. "You—?"

"Yes! It's Simpson! I watched the imp change into Simpson! I defeated him! The imp is finished!" I cried. "As soon as I give him back his tail, he's history! He's going away forever!"

"Wow," Tim muttered, his eyes wide with amazement. "Wow, Sam. I can't believe it!"

"Is that cool, or what?" I said. I raised my free hand to slap him a high five.

But instead, he reached for the tail. "Can I hold it for a second?" he asked. "I just want to hold it."

"Oh. Well . . ." I started to hand it to him.

Then I stopped with a gasp.

And jerked my hand back.

Tim Poster.

Drop the first letter.

Im Poster.

Imp oster.

Imposter!

"No!" I screamed. "You too! You're an imp!"

Tim leaped forward and grabbed the tail. "Give me my brother's tail!"

I let out a gasp. "Huh? Your brother?"

He struggled to grab the tail from my hand.

I swung away from him and slammed hard into the wall.

He tackled me around the waist and sent me toppling to the floor. The tail began to unravel.

"Owwww!"

I cried out as he drove an elbow into my ribs. As I struggled to breathe, he grabbed the tail with both hands.

I made a wild swipe at it—too late.

Tim pulled the tail away from me—and tossed it to someone running toward us fast.

Simpson!

"Give it back!" I screamed. "We made a deal—!"

The two imps tossed back their heads and laughed.

As I pulled myself to my feet, they both changed. They shrank quickly, their clothes disappearing under green skin.

Back to their creature bodies, they scampered up the steps, cackling to each other.

"Come back—!" I lurched after them.

I let out a roar of anger. I was so angry at myself for believing Simpson, for letting him escape.

"I know who you are!" I screamed. "You're both finished here! Do you hear me? I know who you are!"

I reached the top of the staircase—and practically knocked Mr. Kimpall over.

"Sam?" He jumped back in surprise.

"Help me!" I gasped. "There are two of them! Two imps!"

He put a hand on my shoulder. "Calm down, Sam. Take a deep breath, okay?"

"But—but—" I sputtered.

I pulled away from him. "You don't understand! You're letting them get away!"

"Sam, listen to me," he said softly.

Mr. Kimpall.

I stared at him, my chest heaving, heart thudding.

Drop the first letter.

Impall.

Imp all.

"Oh, nooooo!" I moaned. "Mr. Kimpall? You too?"

He nodded coldly. "I'm their dad." And grabbed me by the shoulders. And pressed me against the wall.

"I'm sorry, Sam," he whispered. "But I can't have you ruining things for my whole family. Now you know too much."

"Wh-what are you going to do to me?" I stammered.

"This is *our* school," Mr. Kimpall rasped. "My family has a good thing going here. A nice, easy life. And a new group of victims every school year. This school is the perfect place for an imp family to hide. And we're not going to let *you* ruin it for us!"

He pressed me harder against the wall. He was breathing rapidly, wheezing, his face bright red.

I braced myself against the wall—and gave him a hard kick in the knee.

He uttered a cry and stumbled back.

I took off, running down the hall.

But I didn't get far. The other two imps darted to block my path.

"Hold him there!" Mr. Kimpall ordered, rubbing

his knee. "Don't let him get away."

And then he quickly changed into a green imp creature.

"Look out!" I screamed at the top of my lungs at the other two imps.

I dove between them and kept running.

I ran down the stairs and headed to the auditorium. People were still arriving for the concert. The seats were nearly filled.

I'll be safe there, I decided.

The imps won't follow me inside.

I heard a woman's voice calling me. Ms. Simpkin made her way out of a crowd of parents.

She came running up to me. "Sam? The rest of the band is onstage. Everyone was looking for you."

"The imps—!" I gasped. "I'm so glad to see you! They—they—!" I pointed down the hall. "It's a whole family. Three of them! Please help me! Do something! They—"

And then I stopped with a sharp cry.

Ms. Simpkin.

Drop the first letter.

Impkin.

Imp kin.

"No," I whispered. I started to back away. "No. You're one of them, too!"

Her eyes narrowed on me. Her face began to shrink. She reached for me as her skin turned green and her body transformed.

I saw the other three imps scampering toward me, two of them on all fours. Their tails slapped the floor loudly behind them as they moved.

I grabbed the nearest doorknob and slipped inside. I slammed the door shut behind me.

Where was I?

I heard a hum of voices. Instruments tuning up.

I stepped through a thick gray curtain.

And found myself on the auditorium stage.

Mr. Kelly stood in front of the band. He frowned at me as I staggered across the stage. "Sam—where is your horn?"

I turned to the audience. Were my parents out there?

The bright lights blinded me. I couldn't see any of the faces clearly.

"Sam, get to your place," Mr. Kelly called. "We're going to start.

"Mom? Dad?" I called. "The imps—!"

I heard gasps and startled cries all around.

Spinning around, I saw the four imps shove through the stage door. Tails slapping the wooden floor, they leaped onto the stage after me.

They held hands and formed a tight circle around me. They had me trapped inside the circle.

A hush fell over the audience. They didn't know what to make of this. Was it part of the show?

Were those green creatures actually kids in costumes?

"Somebody help me!" I screamed.

No one moved.

The four imps moved around me. Circling . . . circling.

Their black eyes glared coldly at me. Their tails slapped in rhythm. They snapped their jaws as they walked around and around.

Suddenly, my legs tensed. I felt a shock of energy run up and down my back.

They're using their powers, I realized. They're using their magic on me.

My hands shot up into the air.

I tried to lower them, but I couldn't. They were held high by an invisible force.

Against my will, my legs started to move. My body swayed.

I started to do an awkward dance.

"Help me!" I shouted. "They're making me dance!"

My shoes tapped the floor. My feet moved faster, faster.

Out of control.

I had no control of my body. The imps had taken over.

What did they plan to do? Dance me to death?

My feet tapped the floor. My hands swayed above my head.

I couldn't stop.

The imps grinned as they moved around me. Circling, circling . . . watching my horror as I tapped and twirled.

What would they do to me next?

Whatever it was, I was doomed.

Then I had an idea. A desperate idea.

As I danced, I reached out—and grabbed an imp by the hands. Dancing, dancing frantically, I tugged it to the front of the stage.

"Eeeeee!" The imp howled in surprise. The audience laughed at the strange high-pitched sound.

The imp tried to pull away, but I held tight.

And holding the imp's hands in front of me, I forced it to dance with me.

Kick kick. Kick kick. Sway kick.

I got up on tiptoe and twirled one way, then the other. I kicked and bowed and swayed. And forced the confused imp to follow along.

The auditorium had been silent. But now a few

people started to laugh.

As the imp and I danced, one of the snare drummers began to drum along. Some people started to clap.

More people were laughing now.

The imp frowned at me, desperate to pull free.

But its grip was growing weaker. I could see its color fade. Its eyes grew wide with panic.

Behind us, I saw the other imps step back. Their faces were tight with fear.

They knew what I was doing.

I could feel their power fading. They were losing control of me.

Gripping the imp's hands tightly, I pretended to slip. I fell backward to the floor. The imp fell on top of me.

The audience roared now.

Onstage, kids in the band were laughing, too.

I could see the light fading in the imp's eyes. I could feel its strength ebbing away.

The other imps faded. They appeared to be shrinking, caving in on themselves.

I got up and twirled the imp around in another wild, crazy dance.

The audience laughed louder.

They didn't know that their laughter was my weapon. They didn't know that laughter could kill.

But I remembered my research about imps. I

remembered everything I read about them.

I remembered that they love jokes of all kinds . . . *but they cannot stand to be laughed at*!

I danced crazier and crazier, stomping my shoes on the floor. Tangling my legs. Falling again. Whipping my head from side to side. Twisting and shimmying.

And the audience roared . . .

Roared until the four imps faded away. Laughed as the horrified imps shrank . . . shrank until they were tiny round green puddles on the stage floor.

And then finally, I stopped my dance.

And collapsed to the floor. And listened to the applause, the wild applause.

Applause that I knew I would never forget.

A few days later, Mr. Kelly was named acting principal of the school. That afternoon, he called me to his office.

His expression was solemn as he closed the office door behind us. "First of all, Sam," he began, "I want to congratulate you. You did a real service to Wilton Middle School by destroying the imps."

"Uh . . . thank you," I said awkwardly.

He shook my hand. "That took real courage, Sam," he said softly. "Those imps ran wild for years until you came along. You should be very proud of yourself."

"Thank you," I repeated.

He let go of my hand. "But we have one other lit-tle problem," he said, sighing.

I swallowed. "Problem?"

He nodded. "You see, now that the imps are gone, the *troll* has come out of its hiding place."

Mr. Kelly's eyes locked on mine. "Think you could help us with this one?"

ABOUT THE AUTHOR

R.L. STINE says he has a great job. "My job is to give kids the CREEPS!" With his scary books, R.L. has terrified kids all over the world. He has sold over 300 million books, making him the best-selling children's author in history.

These days, R.L. is dishing out new frights in his series THE NIGHTMARE ROOM. When he isn't working, he likes to read old mysteries, watch *SpongeBob Squarepants* on TV, and take his dog, Nadine, for long walks around New York City, where he lives with his wife, Jane, and son, Matthew.

Take a look at what's ahead in
THE NIGHTMARE ROOM #12
Visitors

"You guys, I've got something so amazing to show you!" I hung my camera around my neck, grabbed my friends Summer and Ben by their arms, and dragged them downstairs.

"Hello, it's nice to see you. Thank you for coming over . . ." Jeff teased. "There are dozens of greetings you could have used, Ben."

"Where are you taking us?" Summer asked.

"Just follow me," I told them. "You've got to see this for yourselves."

I led them outside. It was a beautiful, clear night. I paused in the backyard to gaze up at the sky. There were millions of stars and planets.

Which ones had aliens living on them? Which ones had sent visitors to Earth?

We flicked on our flashlights and started into the woods. There was no wind that night. Everything was very still.

"It's kind of spooky out here," Jeff whispered.

We walked for about ten minutes. I hoped I could find my way back to the figure eight. What if I couldn't? Jeff and Summer would never believe anything I had to say then.

"How much farther?" Summer asked. "It feels like we've been walking forever."

"Are you sure you know how to get back?" Jeff asked.

"We won't get lost," I promised. "I think we're almost there."

A few minutes later, I stepped into the clearing.

There was the figure eight. The moon had risen, and the figure seemed to glow in the moonlight.

"This is it," I told them. Even though it was dark, I lifted my camera and snapped a few pictures.

Summer and Jeff stared at it. Summer rolled her eyes. "Here we go again," she mumbled. Then she turned to me.

"This is it?" she echoed. "What's it?"

"The figure eight!" I cried. "Look it at! It's huge! Something burned it into the grass!"

Summer and Jeff stepped closer. "So?" Summer said.

"Don't you think it's mysterious?" I cried. "I mean, how did it get here? Who made it? Why?"

"It's just smushed-down grass," Jeff said.

"Step inside it!" I dared them. "Just step over that line. You'll see."

"You go first," Jeff said to Summer.

"Wimp," Summer muttered. She stepped across

the line in the grass and stood inside one of the loops of the eight.

I waited for her body to jolt the way mine had.

But she just stood there calmly.

"Come on in, Jeff," she said. "There's nothing to be afraid of."

Jeff stepped inside the loop. Nothing happened to him, either.

"Don't you feel anything?" I asked them. "Don't you feel the power?"

"Ben, stop it," Summer pleaded. "You're really scaring me."

"Look!" I moved carefully toward the figure eight. I hesitated because I wasn't eager to get shocked again.

I stepped quickly over the line.

Zzzip!

I felt a sharp shock and jumped right back out.

"Did you see that?" I demanded.

"I saw you jump," Jeff said. "But I already knew you could do that."

"You don't feel a shock or anything?" I cried.

"Ben, is this supposed to be another alien thing?" Summer asked.

"Well—"

"All you think about is aliens," Jeff said. "You see signs of them everywhere!"

"Face it. You're obsessed," Summer said. She

paused and looked me straight in the eye. "Ben, you're starting to sound really crazy."

My jaw fell open. "How can you say that?" I asked. "You guys are my best friends!"

They exchanged that look again. My heart sank. If I couldn't count on Summer and Jeff, who could I count on? I was beginning to feel so alone.

Then I heard something. A rustle.

I glanced up at the treetops. The air was dead calm. Not a breath of wind.

I froze, listening. Something rustled again.

"Did you hear that?" I whispered.

"Now what?" Summer said. "Are the aliens landing?"

"Sshhh!" I held one hand up to shush her. We all stood still.

Behind us, a twig snapped. I heard feet shuffling through the leaves.

"*Now* did you hear something?" I whispered.

Summer and Jeff nodded.

There was someone else in the woods!

I ran toward the sound. Whoever was out there, I was going to catch him—or her, or it.

"Ben, what are you doing?" Summer called. She and Jeff hurried after me.

I dashed into the woods. I heard footsteps running away from me, back toward my house.

The moonlight filtered through the tall trees. I

flipped on my flashlight. I stopped for a second to listen.

Someone was running to my left. I ran in that direction, my flashlight beaming.

I was getting closer. I could hear the person breathing heavily.

"Who's there?" I called.

No one answered.

At last I got close enough to catch a glimpse. The beam of my flashlight grazed the back of the person's head.

I saw a flash of blue. Bright blue. A glowing, bright blue.

A roaring boom—like thunder—made me gasp.

An alien!

It was finally happening. I was chasing an alien!

"Come back!" I shouted. "I just want to talk to you! I won't hurt you!"

The flash of blue vanished behind a clump of tall bushes.

"Please—come back!"

I dove into the bushes. My feet tangled in a long, twisting vine.

With a cry, I fell to the ground.

My heart thudding, I scrambled quickly to my feet. I searched for the eerie, blue color. Listened for footsteps.

No. The alien had disappeared.

Summer and Jeff caught up with me. "Did you see that? A flash of blue!"

They shook their heads. "We heard someone running," Summer said. "But we didn't see anyone."

"But did you hear that boom?" I went on. "It sounded like thunder. And look! It's perfectly clear tonight. There are no clouds in the sky!"

"Calm down, Ben," Jeff said. "Maybe it was a sonic boom from one of those new jets at the military base in Roswell."

"Maybe," I replied. "But the flash of blue light— it's one of the signs."

"Signs of what?" Summer asked. "Of Ben Shipley losing his mind?"

"One of the signs of alien life," I said. "I'm not crazy, you two. First that weird figure eight. Then the flash of blue..."

They started back toward the house. My mind spinning, I hurried to keep up with them.

Summer and Jeff didn't say much. I could tell I was freaking them out.

I'm not losing my mind, I thought. I know I'm right.

I saw an alien tonight. It *had* to be an alien!